A Season of Love

Kim Watters

HARLEQUIN® LOVE INSPIRED®

Recycling programs for this product may not exist in your area.

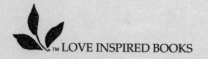 LOVE INSPIRED BOOKS

ISBN-13: 978-0-373-81724-5

A SEASON OF LOVE

www.Harlequin.com

Printed in U.S.A.

Though you have made me see troubles,
many and bitter, you will restore my life again; from
the depths of the earth you will again bring me up.
—*Psalms* 71:20

For Shane and Emily, who continue to supply me with endless children's anecdotes that occasionally make their way into my stories.

For my parents, who instilled the pleasure of reading into me at an early age and taught me to believe that I could do anything.

For my sister, who introduced me to Harlequin stories.

For Marc, who kept me on track and sane while writing this book.

For Linda and Kerrie, critique partners extraordinaire.

And a special thanks to Evvere Anthony, who patiently answered all my questions.

Chapter One

Another Christmas carol drifted through the airwaves and settled on Holly Stanwyck's shoulders as she sat in her deserted shop. Normally the music would soothe her, but not today. She needed some customers to walk through the front door of 'Tis Always the Season and buy enough merchandise to pay for the day's overhead expenses. Without being able to put out new offerings in the past few weeks, though, the odds of that happening were nil.

Taking a break from the computer, she opened her mail and stared at another past-due notice before she placed it in the manila folder with the others. The real meaning of Christmas and the reason for the store had died two years ago, along with her dreams of a happily ever after.

"Bah, humbug." Holly never thought she'd utter those words. Fisting her palms, she rested her chin against them and stared out at the tree behind the wrought-iron fence, its bare limbs scarcely darker than the clouds spitting snowflakes. Even the cold marble pillars and structure of the courthouse in the center of the square seemed to shrink under the weight of the early November storm. She blew her wispy bangs from her eyes.

She missed her husband. The store had been his idea; a way to keep Christmas in their hearts all year round and a way to sell the hand-carved wooden crosses, ornaments, figurines and crèches he made in the workshop behind their bungalow, along with other Christmas merchandise. Only one of his masterpieces remained, and with Jared dead, no new ones would grace the shelves.

In a few moments, she regained her composure and breathed in the scent of cinnamon wafting from the candle on the shelf behind her head. It reminded her of her grandmother's house in the suburbs of Chicago, and she envisioned Nana Marie's soft arms cocooning her in comfort. *There is nothing in life that you can't handle, child. Just put your trust in the Lord, and everything will be all right.*

Easier said than done. She didn't believe anymore and only went through the motions for her twelve-year-old son, Cameron. Still, Holly

Stanwyck was no quitter. She would not lose everything she and Jared had worked so hard for. The new business venture she'd thought of last night would work. Refocusing on the words on the computer screen, she felt hope blaze through her. She'd get caught up on her bills and give Cam the Christmas he longed for.

Where was Cameron anyway? She glanced at her watch and her heart sank. School had ended an hour ago. If he didn't show up in the next few minutes, she'd have to close up the shop and go searching for him again.

The bell above the door jingled. Quickly stuffing the folder under the counter, she stood and plastered on a smile, hoping her customer wouldn't see the desperation lingering in her eyes. "Welcome to 'Tis Always..." Her words died in her throat as the door shut.

A tall, dark-haired stranger stood behind her son, and the scowl on the man's face didn't bode well. Cam had obviously forgotten their numerous talks about stranger danger, even in the small town. But then again, from first impressions, she guessed Cam didn't have much of a choice. Knots formed in her stomach. This wasn't a social visit. What had her son done now?

The man's drab olive military-style coat did little to hide his muscular frame and only accentuated his height. Snowflakes clung to his cropped dark hair and dusted his jacket, but a few hugged his long eyelashes, outlining incredible but unsettling sapphire-blue eyes. His lips had yet to break into a fraction of a smile. She straightened her shoulders, refusing to be intimidated by him as she concentrated on her son.

"Cameron." She glanced at her watch again. "Where have you been?" Trying to keep the censure from her voice and keep her tone light, she failed miserably. "Thank you for bringing him back, Mr...."

"You're welcome. It's Pellegrino. Ethan Pellegrino." He spoke as if she should recognize his name. His lips formed a straight line and fatigue bracketed his eyes. He took his left hand off her son's shoulder and put it in his pocket, but not before fisting and then flexing his fingers.

Holly racked her brain but came up empty. She would remember meeting him, although his name did sound vaguely familiar now, as if she'd seen it written down somewhere in the recent past.

"Holly Stanwyck." Holly had enough manners to jut her hand out. The man didn't reciprocate. He stared at her outstretched hand and shifted his weight. How rude. Holly let her hand drop back to the counter.

After a few uncomfortable seconds, she

picked up a pen and twirled it in her fingers. Glancing past his broad shoulders, she noticed the steady stream of snowflakes increasing outside the front window. More anxiety tightened the knots inside her. If the snow continued, she'd have to drag out the shovel by nightfall and, worse, drive in it. But that was probably going to be the least of her worries. What had Cameron done now that this Ethan Pellegrino had to bring him to the shop?

"Pleased to meet you, Mr. Pellegrino." *I think.* She glanced at the frown hugging her son's lips. "What's going on?" Her words added another layer to the growing tension. Uneasy, she walked to the other side of the counter, put her arm around her son and pulled him to her. At the man's immobile expression, her nerves threatened to dislodge the glass of water she'd drunk earlier.

"Your son should tell you."

"Cameron?" Her son pulled away, hung his head and then kicked at an imaginary spot on the floor. "What have you been up to?" She clipped her words and tried to remain unemotional, but failed. Cameron had been getting into trouble a lot lately.

Who was this stranger residing in her son's body? He looked the same with his unruly dark blond hair and blue eyes, but his attitude had gone south. She needed to get a handle on it because in the next year or so, he'd be taller than she'd be. And more opinionated and more uncontrollable. The pen in her hand bent under the pressure.

"I took the long way here."

She ground her teeth as a scowl twisted Cam's lips. "With Patrick?"

"Why do you care who I walk with?"

Her son's new friend was bad news, but the more Holly brought that fact up, the more Cameron hung out with him instead of his other friends. Her grip tightened. She'd lost Jared two years earlier, and she was going to lose the store in a few months if things didn't improve. She couldn't lose Cameron, as well. "I care because I love you."

Her son's scowl deepened and he moved away when she tried to push his bangs from his eyes. "I don't see why you won't let me take the bus *home* after school. Everyone else does."

Holly sighed, refraining from the age-old saying of asking if everyone jumped off a bridge, would he follow? "Because I'm not there, I'm here, and you didn't want to go to the YMCA. And now there's apparently a good reason you're to come here, that's why."

"The YMCA is for babies. Why did Dad have to die?" Cam threw his backpack down and crossed his arms over his chest. "If he were alive, you'd be at home like Matt's or Tyler's mom."

At least she understood where the anger came from now. Communicating with her son lately had been harder than talking to the accounts-receivable people trying to collect on her past-due invoices. "Cam—I…"

Ethan Pellegrino shifted his weight, reminding Holly they weren't alone. Her shoulders sagged. Now was not the time to have a heart-to-heart talk with her son about the fact that even if his father were alive, she'd still work outside the home as she'd always done. She had no choice now, and once she faced the reality that the store would be going out of business soon, she'd have to find another job to pay her bills. She'd been a bookkeeper before and could do it again, but she'd deal with that later. "What were you doing that Mr. Pellegrino felt compelled to bring you here?"

"Patrick and I were having some fun."

"Fun?" Holly sank against the counter and rubbed her forehead. Her shoulder muscles tightened, creating an instant headache. "You know I don't want you hanging around him. Thanks for bringing him to me, Mr. Pellegrino. I can take it from here."

The man crossed his arms, pursed his lips

and glowered at her son. "Not until I hear him utter the truth about where he was and what he was doing."

"Excuse me?" Holly shoved her hands onto her hips and bit back her anger as she glared at Ethan Pellegrino. Somehow she'd lost control of the situation. "You don't trust that I can deal with whatever *my* son has done?"

"It's not you. It's him. I doubt he'll tell you the truth. I'm familiar with teenagers."

"It's not like we did much damage," Cameron shot back.

"Cameron. Show some respect." Holly corrected her son. "You will not speak to an adult that way no matter what the situation is. Understood?"

Cam nodded and stared at the floor.

"Now, what did Cameron and Patrick do?"

"They spray painted my garage door." The man scraped his hand through his short hair as his gaze penetrated hers.

Cam had picked the wrong person to mess with.

Bile caught in her throat. Cameron had gone too far this time. The chat with the principal this morning had confirmed her son was heading down the wrong path. Holly felt powerless and overwhelmed by his attitude and change in personality. Inhaling sharply, she fought for control.

She was out of ideas on how to break through the wall Cameron had built around himself lately. Where communication had been easy when he was young, the moment he turned twelve and hormones kicked in, he'd turned inward and quit talking to her other than a few grunts here and there or to ask for money. "You spray painted Mr. Pellegrino's garage? Why?"

"Because I wanted to." Underneath all of Cameron's bravado, Holly sensed him ready to implode. His eyes flashed with anger, hurt and panic, emotions she identified with on a daily basis.

Tagging was a minor offense in Dynamite Creek, Arizona, and usually had some kind of monetary fine—something she couldn't afford right now. "That's not a good enough answer. I believe both Mr. Pellegrino and I deserve to know the truth."

Out of the corner of her eye, she watched the man shift his weight and continue to flex his hand as if testing out its strength while he glanced around the store.

"Because I heard that *he's* going to evict us. This is Dad's place. He can't do that."

"What? Where did you hear that?" The gnawing sensation took hold in her stomach and refused to let go as the realization hit. Mr. Pellegrino owned the building. She'd never met her landlord because he was supposed to be in Afghanistan. Jared had set everything up, and the past two years she'd signed the contracts with someone named Nan Emrey on the owner's behalf.

She knew she'd have to deal with her rent issues sooner rather than later, but she'd thought it would be with Nan, not the six-foot male taking up more space in her shop than she was comfortable with. And now, thanks to Cameron, that time had probably come; not that her son was responsible for her failure to pay the rent. The place Jared envisioned all through college and during their early married lives was about to disappear. More sadness consumed her. 'Tis Always the Season was one of the few remaining ties they had to Jared.

She stared into Mr. Pellegrino's immobile expression and shivered before she broke contact and refocused on her son.

"I heard it from Delany Wilson." Anger choked his voice and emotion hovered in his eyes. "She told the whole class. She said we were going to lose everything—the business, the house, our car—and end up living out of a grocery cart in the park across the street."

"That's not true, Cam." They weren't in danger of losing the house yet, because Holly had paid her mortgage and her maxed-out home-equity loan before her rent. "Mr. Pellegrino is not going to evict us from our house. Only the bank can do that. I promise you, though, no matter what happens we will not be living out of a grocery cart."

Holly had no idea what the future held in store for them. She did know that even if they had to eventually walk away from the house, they would not be homeless; both she and Jared had family in Tucson. She'd refused to let Cam know about all the money problems because she wanted to let him remain a child for a bit longer. Maybe she was doing him a disservice.

Cam wiped his nose on his jacket sleeve. Holly didn't correct his actions, hoping he didn't realize that she hadn't mentioned anything about the store. A quick glance at her landlord confirmed he'd caught on to her son's words, and their gazes met and held a few seconds before he glanced away. She knew this conversation was far from over, but she hoped Ethan wouldn't bring up the issue in front of her son. She had enough to deal with.

"Promise?"

"Promise. Why didn't you come to me, Cam?"

"Because I can't talk to you. You're always

distracted. Or worried. Or busy." Cameron pursed his lips and flailed his arms.

Holly wanted to deny it, but she couldn't. Truth became claws of pain that ripped apart what remained of her heart. In spending so much time worrying about the house and the shop, she'd lost focus of her son.

Pulling Cam to her again, she put her arms around him and held him gently, cradling him. "I'm so sorry, honey. I—I don't— I'm sorry." Holly just stood and held her son. A tear slid from beneath her closed eyes. Cam squeezed her back, his thin body reminding her that he was just a child who needed help in understanding what happened around him.

Ethan cleared his throat. Holly still had to deal with the situation that had brought him here in the first place. No matter what Cameron was going through, she couldn't condone his behavior and needed to get a handle on it quickly before it spun further out of control.

Releasing her son, she lifted his chin and stared into his unhappy eyes. "I'm still upset by your actions at Mr. Pellegrino's house. You know what you did was wrong."

"Yes," Cam agreed halfheartedly.

"Good. And you know there's going to be a consequence."

"But—"

"No buts." After wiping her hands on her jeans, she glanced at her landlord, surprised to see such compassion before his expression closed. "We're going to Mr. Pellegrino's house this weekend to remove the graffiti. Patrick, too, as soon as I talk to his parents."

"That won't be necessary."

Holly took a step back and openly stared at the man. With his arms now folded across his chest and his legs spread shoulder-width apart, she deemed him another force to be reckoned with. The tick in his jawline and the immobile line of his lips didn't help, either.

"It is necessary." She placed her hands on Cam's shoulders and spun him around to face the man. "My son needs to be held responsible for his actions. Why else would you have brought him here if you didn't want some sort of resolution, Mr. Pellegrino?"

"Please, call me Ethan. Point taken. I'll stop by tomorrow to set up the details." He rubbed the stubble on his chin and stared at her baldly. But it was the words he didn't say that concerned Holly. Her gut told her that when Mr. Pellegrino—no, Ethan—came by tomorrow, he'd have her eviction notice ready to add to the pile of past-due invoices underneath her counter.

* * *

"Welcome to 'Tis Always the Season." Holly glanced up from her computer the next day. When she saw who stood at the threshold of her shop, her heart began to beat rapidly inside her chest.

"Afternoon." Ethan Pellegrino took up more space than he should. A small gust of wind carried in the snowflakes and made her shiver, but that wasn't what stole her breath away and froze her spine into a straight line. Crossing her arms, she leaned against the counter.

His expression matched the snow-laden clouds in the sky behind him. Not surprising, since she knew the nature of his visit today. She'd been expecting him, but that still didn't make today's conversation any easier.

Ethan rubbed his left hand over his five-o'clock shadow and broke eye contact for a moment. Hesitation danced over his features as he let out a sigh. "I won't sugarcoat the situation. I was going to come by at the end of the week. Yesterday's incident made it that much sooner. You know I'm here to collect the past-due rent as well as talk about the garage."

Holly stared at a bare spot on the counter. Heat stung her cheeks, and humiliation draped across her until the butterflies in her stomach begged for release. Four months behind in rent and more than one hundred and twenty days past due on most of her invoices, it had only been a matter of time. She'd just hoped she could get through Christmas and figure out another game plan before she had to close. "I know. Thanks for not bringing it up in front of Cam yesterday."

"I'd like to think I have more tact than that."

Her newly designed flyers on the counter caught her attention. Her idea was a good one, and people would hire her. People who came into the shop told her she had a flair for decorating, and she'd learned quite a bit from all the classes she'd taken at the local community college when they'd talked about opening the store. In about an hour, Cameron would come sullenly through the doors after school, and she'd had hopes they could fold, stuff and stamp the envelopes after he'd finished his homework. Unless Ethan gave her a reprieve, they'd have to scrounge boxes from the local market instead.

"I'm sorry. I don't have the rent. But I'm working on it. I just need a bit more time." Her voice squeaked and her fingers gripped the counter until her knuckles gleamed white. Jared had died with a life-insurance policy in place, but that had been eaten up by both their medical bills from the car accident, and things had been tough these past two years despite the social-security benefits. The rent due to Ethan had gone toward her mortgage payments, and the payments to her vendors had gone to her utility bills.

His expression remained detached. Unless he held her stuff as collateral, she could still sell the merchandise online and coordinate her decorating services from her home. It wouldn't be easy, but it was the only fair thing to do. He needed a renter who could pay the rent, and it would be easier for her to not have to worry about it anymore. But to give up Jared's dream... It would give her more time to focus on her son. She knew what she had to do even though the words were hard to form. "I'll vacate immediately."

A kaleidoscope of emotions flickered across his features but didn't match his words. "How much time do you need?"

Closing her eyes for a brief second, and knowing this was for the best, Holly shuddered at the thought of boxing everything up. Jared's hopes and dreams packed into a dark world and crowded together, lifeless, with no one to enjoy them. She fingered the carved baby Jesus ornament by the old-fashioned cash register that Jared had given her the day they'd opened the store, determination filling her every movement.

She would find everything in the store a new

home and maybe bring in enough money to pay her mortgage and provide her son with a Christmas present this year. Straightening her shoulders, she flipped her hair back and met his gaze. "Well, if I can run a going-out-of-business sale for a few weeks, that should help. The rest I'll auction off online, along with the trees and fixtures. Today's November 3. Can I have until the end of the month?"

"Isn't this supposed to be your busy season?" When Ethan used both hands to pick up the Santa snow globe from the counter and shake it, Holly noticed the scars covering his entire right hand and disappearing under his sleeve. When she saw the nubs where his fingers should have been, she bit her bottom lip. Now she understood his hesitation yesterday about shaking her hand. More heat claimed her cheeks, because she'd assumed he was being rude. What had happened? And did she really want to know?

Yes… No. Holly warred with her answer as compassion filled her. The scars looked fresh, but she didn't have the time or the energy to open another place in her heart right now. Cameron and her money issues took up just about everything she had. She looked away, and from inside the globe, the jovial old man, the commercial epitome of the season, mocked her with his sack of presents. "It should be, but nothing's been *busy* since the economy went south."

Staring at the bits of white swirling around in the liquid inside the glass, Holly was reminded of her life right now. Drifting along but spiraling downward, resting at the bottom until someone came along and shook things up.

Like Ethan.

Not that she could blame him. Business was business.

When Ethan shook the globe again, she caught him looking at her over the top of the smooth glass. Lines were etched into the skin framing his deep blue eyes, but she sensed he had nothing to laugh about these days, either.

Her breath stalled, leaving her struggling to push away the strange, forgotten emotion gripping her heart. Moments passed before she managed to blink and break the effect he had on her. The snowflakes he'd carried in with him had melted, creating drops of water that glistened in his short, dark, wavy hair and on his jacket. Her instincts were to dust off the moisture so he wouldn't catch a cold, but she refrained from leaning across the counter and touching him with anything but her gaze. A day's growth of beard hugged the contours of his strong jaw, the intensity of his expression broken by his slight frown.

"What are these flyers for?" Ethan set the snow globe back on the counter, picked one up, then stared at the words.

Releasing her breath, Holly refocused on what should be the most important thing to her right now—making an income to pay her bills. "It's an advertisement for a holiday home-decorating service for people who are too busy to do it themselves this time of year."

"That's an interesting concept." Ethan looked around the store pensively. An awkward moment passed between them as another Christmas carol filled the air. "Will it bring in enough money for you to get caught up?"

Holly found herself staring back into Ethan's blue eyes and felt a current threatening to pull her under. She floundered, trying to free herself from its grasp. Ethan Pellegrino confused her. She shrugged to relieve the tension building in her shoulders and arms. "Honestly? I have no idea, but I have to try."

The wind kicked up beyond the glass door, which protected them from the cold, even though the temperature seemed to drop inside. She shivered and pulled her black sweater tighter. Snow started to accumulate on the lawn across the street. Maybe she'd close up shop early and try to make it home once Cameron arrived from school. It wasn't as if she'd have much business this afternoon anyway, and they could take care of the flyers anywhere.

Ethan scraped his good hand through his hair and contemplated his next move. What was another month in the scheme of things? The thirty-six-hundred dollars was just a drop in the bucket of what he needed to operate his dog sanctuary, bring rescued dogs over from Afghanistan and introduce them to, or in some cases reunite them with, their new owners. "You can stay until the end of the year."

How could he kick her out before Christmas? Not only would he have a hard time reconciling that with God, Ethan also had his mom to contend with. She wouldn't take too kindly to him evicting the woman during the holidays.

"Thank you."

Ethan looked away from Holly's open expression and soft, feminine features to stare at the scars on his hand where his fingers used to be. He'd been one of the lucky ones. Along with the chaplain he was assigned to protect, two of his other comrades in the convoy in Afghanistan had been killed; one of them had been a father and the other a newlywed.

Why the Lord chose those three to die mystified Ethan. If anyone should have been called home, it should have been him. Nobody depended on him or needed him. If anything, he needed someone else since returning home from rehab. Buttoning a shirt and learning to write with his left hand continued to challenge him. Determination forced its way past the dissatisfaction as he shifted and flexed his injured hand. God had a plan for him, and it revolved around the new canine shelter.

"It's not a problem." Ethan would find the money owed from the rent elsewhere, especially since in his gut, he knew Holly wouldn't ever get caught up. Someone said charity began at home. Well, right now this was as close to home as he was going to get. He could still advertise for a renter, but with the three other storefronts available along the main square, it might take a while. As long as Holly made her utilities, what difference was it going to make? Peace settled inside him as he feigned interest again in the snow globe.

Dark blond hair fell to her shoulders and framed her pale face, accentuating the dark circles under her green eyes. The black sweater she clutched around her only made her appear more fragile, as did the fact she barely came up to his shoulder. A light dusting of freckles endeared her to him more than he was comfortable with.

The woman looked as if she needed a break right now. The urge to shelter and protect her almost brought him to his knees. While his stint as an army chaplain's assistant had come to an end, he couldn't help who he was. He needed to think of something else.

"So your last name is Stanwyck. I knew a Jared Stanwyck. Any relation?"

When Holly nodded, his hope chose a quick exit.

"My late husband."

His mom had told him about Jared's car accident a few years back, but she'd failed to mention he'd left behind a wife and son. Another reason he couldn't evict her any sooner than the end of the year. "I'm sorry for your loss."

"Thanks. How did you know him?"

At her lost expression, his heartbeat accelerated. He picked up the carved wooden ornament sitting by the cash register. It was better than the similar one Jared had done in high school during shop class, but he'd recognize the talent anywhere. "We grew up a few blocks from each other and played ball together in school, but pretty much lost touch after graduation. I went into the military. He went to Northern Arizona University." He stared at her and then his injured hand. "If anyone… Never mind. I see Jared's work got better."

"It did. I used to have a lot of his stuff here, but it's all sold, except for one of his earlier pieces. I'm sorry for your loss, as well."

"Thanks." Ethan put the figurine back down and his attention strayed to the empty fireplace along the wall, where she'd hung a few stockings, with more placed in the nook built beside it. The store had a pleasant feel and smell to it. As soon as he finished with the dog areas, he could use some advice on how to decorate the reception area he had in mind for Beyond the Borders Dog Sanctuary so it would look nice when he welcomed owners either dropping off or picking up their dogs.

He sniffed in the scent of cinnamon and listened to the sound of another Christmas carol coming over the speakers behind the counter. Lights twinkled on various-size fake trees, each pine with its own different theme. Larger ornaments interspersed with snowflakes hung from the ceiling, and wreaths of all sizes hung on the walls. Shelves lined the back walls, but even from here, Ethan could see they lacked merchandise.

He sensed Holly was in more financial distress than just behind in her rent and wondered if she was even going to make it through the holidays. The closer he inspected the store, the more gaps he found on the trees, shelves and walls. Would her last-ditch effort to set up decorations for other people work?

He hoped so. Even though he needed the rent

money for his shelter, it wouldn't be coming from here. He'd already made up his mind and couldn't immediately evict his friend's widow. What a mess. He refocused on the snow globe with the Santa figure. Picking it up, he shook it again, creating a flurry of activity inside. The turbulence suited his mood.

"How much is this?"

"Twenty-four ninety-nine. I have others if you'd like to see them. They're right this way."

Holly had no idea why she prolonged Ethan's visit. She should be shooing him out the door so she could free herself from his closeness and plan her going-out-of-business strategy before Cameron showed up. Somehow she knew Ethan wasn't quite ready to leave yet, and all of a sudden she wanted his company to chase away the loneliness inside the shop.

Staring at the shelf along the back wall that contained what was left of her snow-globe merchandise, she wondered why the pretty glass orbs were her favorites. Was it because of the intricate work inside? The bright colors in some, the muted colors in others? The idea that each time she shook up the make-believe snow, she created a new scene?

She picked up one with a happy family opening presents on Christmas morning inside. Turning the key on the bottom, she wound the music box, shook the globe and set it back on the shelf, the strains of "We Wish You a Merry Christmas" keeping time with the swirling snow.

Ethan stirred next to her. He obviously wasn't comfortable with her choice, either.

He picked up one containing the manger scene. Ethan fumbled for a moment as he tried to turn the crank on the bottom to listen to the music inside, but without his fingers, the task was impossible until he flipped it into his injured hand and used the good one to start the music.

"What happened to your hand?"

Disgust, sadness and resignation flickered through his eyes as he looked at her, but his expression remained immobile. Holly forgot to breathe. In that quick instant his pain was her own—the death of a dream, a shattered life struggling to mend, a man trying to continue on as if nothing had happened, and yet in a flash everything had changed.

She knew it well. "I'm sorry. Forget that I asked."

"It's okay, Holly. You're not the first to ask and you won't be the last." Setting the snow globe back down on the shelf, Ethan pulled up the sleeve of his dress shirt, exposing more scarring that went to his elbow. "It looks a lot better than it did a few months ago. I served as an army chaplain's assistant in Afghanistan."

"What's that?" Holly never took her eyes off the man's arm. She wasn't repulsed, but she wasn't comfortable, either. Some people wore their scars on the outside, others on the inside and others in both ways.

"I was a bodyguard to whatever chaplain I was assigned to. This time it was a pastor, but I've protected rabbis and priests. We were heading out from our base camp when our convoy encountered a roadside IED. I was one of the lucky ones. The chaplain and two soldiers were killed along with two innocent civilians."

"What's an IED?"

"Improvised explosive device. It's technical words for a bomb."

"I'm so sorry. That must have been horrible for you." Holly knew there was more to the story than just the spoken words, yet she dared not ask. Having closed off her emotions after Jared's death, Holly refused to let them open up again.

"I saw a lot of horrible things over there." Ethan looked as if he wanted to say more about that subject, but his expression closed again and she could almost see his thoughts shift. She braced herself for the next topic of why he was in the store. "Now, about the garage. I'll expect Cameron at eight."

"That works for me, but Cameron will be a bit testy that early in the morning."

"He's almost a teenager. I wouldn't expect anything less. It will be good for him." Ethan cracked a smile and studied the manger inside the snow globe again. "I'll take this one."

"But you don't have to buy anything."

"I don't have to—I want to." Back at the counter, he handed her his credit card, giving Holly her fourth transaction of the day. It wouldn't meet her overhead, but it would help cover something. When she went to wrap it up, he put his good hand on her arm, causing her heart to flutter. "It's a gift for you. We all have troubles, Holly. Sometimes it helps to know that we don't have to carry them alone."

Chapter Two

What had Ethan been thinking? Holly needed money, not a manger scene inside a snow globe. The irony that they were both in the same position but for different reasons would have struck him as funny if things weren't so complicated. Somehow, though, the action seemed right. For a moment, he saw behind her mask of exhaustion and fear and glimpsed the beautiful, caring, compassionate and vulnerable woman underneath.

The kind of woman Jared would fall for. He could, too, if that was what he wanted.

But wanting to protect her when he had to be part of her problem? Sure, he hadn't been the cause of her financial woes, but deep down he knew that being behind in her bills bothered her and he felt like a cad. His mom would have never gone over there and asked for the back rent. As soon as he met Holly Stanwyck, he knew he wasn't going to get it from her. Even if she did somehow come up with it, he wasn't sure he would take it and hoped her idea for the holiday decorating service panned out because she needed money.

The woman also needed some divine intervention right now. He'd add her to his prayers tonight and ask his mother to do the same. Knowing Nan, though, Holly was already on the list.

He slammed his car door shut. As a career soldier forced out because of his injuries, he'd never make it in the civilian world if he didn't toughen up. Right. He was just a big softy, regardless of which side he was on. He'd always had pieces of candy in his pocket for the Afghan children and biscuits for the stray dogs. Now he was opening a sanctuary for dogs to stay while their owners served on foreign soil and to help transport stray dogs adopted by servicemen overseas and reunite them stateside.

Head down to keep the lingering snowflakes from his eyes, and hands bunched inside his coat pockets, he headed toward home and the kennels in the enclosed porch of his house in town that he used as the temporary sanctuary. The permanent one was going to be at his family's farmhouse outside of town, but it needed to be refurbished before he could take the dogs out there. He needed money to do that; some of it he'd hoped to get from Holly. Now he'd have to look elsewhere, since his disability checks barely covered anything.

The lemon scent of cleaner and varied barks greeted him when he walked through the double French doors off the back porch.

"How'd it go?" Meredith, his cousin and fellow board member of Beyond the Borders Dog Sanctuary, greeted him.

"As well as I suspected. There won't be any funds coming from the store anytime soon."

"I'm sorry to hear that. Holly's such a nice woman. She's just had a lot to deal with lately."

Ethan didn't bother to mention the incident with the garage door, seeing as he suspected Meredith was the one who had leaked the eviction information to the wrong person. He loved his cousin, but after being away so long, he'd forgotten her fondness for spreading gossip.

"Anything new with the little girl?" Ethan changed the subject. He didn't want to think about Holly anymore, or the tangible energy that had made the short hairs on the back of his neck stand at attention when his hand grazed hers as he gave her the snow globe. Meredith sat inside the kennel, stroking the little black-and-white mutt's head, and he saw the bandages covering both front legs where the dog had licked away all her fur.

"Pudding Cup will be fine. It's just nerves. She misses her mom."

"How about the big guy I brought in to Tim?" He'd found the injured stray mix huddled on the side of the road yesterday, and it reminded him of one of the dogs their patrol had rescued from the cruelty of an Afghan family. He couldn't ignore the mutt and had thoughts about keeping him, despite the fact Ethan needed to stick to his mission statement. There were other shelters in the area that took in homeless and abandoned dogs.

"He's going to be just fine. Tim thinks he's found a home for him already, so he said not to worry about the bill." Meredith was engaged to the local veterinarian, who also sat on the board and was willing to take care of any of their animals for cost.

"I'll have to stop by and thank him." And make sure the animal was going to a good home. Okay, so he was a sucker for dogs and kids and apparently widows behind on their rent.

Ethan rubbed his hand across his stubbly chin. "Anything else?"

"Yep." Meredith rose to her feet, causing Pudding Cup to whimper and follow her to the gate. "Another stray is being shipped over from

Afghanistan, courtesy of your buddy Phil, along with the other one. Duggan and Jasper arrive Saturday, as do two more dogs on Wednesday. Their owners ship out next Friday."

"Great." Ethan wiped the snowflake residue from his face. His six temporary accommodations were more than full. With four more dogs coming in, he would be over capacity at seven, even though the two from Afghanistan would only be temporary until he could reunite them with their owners, who'd arrived home from their tour of duty last month. He could spill out into his living room, but he'd be over the limit and need a kennel license that much sooner. "Where am I going to put them?"

"Whose brilliant idea was it to provide a home for displaced animals when their owners left?"

"Mine, and you know it's a good one. It's one less thing for our local service men and women to think about while they're doing their tour. Most are fortunate to have family to take care of them, but not all." Ethan had started his studies to be a lay minister and had often counseled some of the enlisted men when the need arose. Leaving their pets behind ranked pretty high up there behind family, especially when they had to dump their companion in a shelter.

Being distracted could get a person killed. He knew that firsthand.

He stared at the nubs on his hand and tried to feel the forgiveness. The emotion refused to come. Five people died that day, and he wrestled with the guilt. Despite the fact he was assigned to protect the chaplain, he felt a responsibility to everyone he traveled with. He should have seen the IED. He knew the signs to look for. A strange vehicle on the side of the road, the wink of light reflecting off the camera lens set up to film the incident, the uneasy feeling harbored inside his gut because of the delay in getting the convoy started.

But he'd been distracted.

None of that mattered now.

What mattered as he stared at his scars and searched for forgiveness was that God had a plan for him. And it revolved around the sanctuary and taking care of man's best friend.

"You're just a bleeding-heart softy. That's what I love about you." Meredith gave him a hug. "I'll take Pudding Cup with me. I like the little girl, and Tim says it's no problem for me to drop her off at his office during the day. I think she'll recover quicker from her abandonment issues, so that frees up one kennel and then you'll have enough."

"Thanks. I appreciate that." For what seemed

the first time that day, he smiled. Meredith was more like a sister than a cousin, and with a job in sales and marketing, she was an invaluable part of the team he'd selected for the board. He'd also asked her fiancé, Tim, and his mom because she owned the property that would house the permanent sanctuary. He should find one other person, to make the numbers odd in case they needed a tiebreaker, and he had yet to find someone with accounting experience so he could concentrate on the dogs and managing the sanctuary.

Things had happened so quickly. He'd probably gone about this the wrong way by accepting animals before he was ready, but the alternative would have been for his first resident, Sadie, to end up in the pound. It would work out. God's plan had been revealed to him during those long hours in the hospital and continued to be revealed daily.

Pudding Cup treated him to a good licking when he bent and scratched her behind her ears. Bear, the black Lab who had alerted him to yesterday's graffiti artists, whined and pawed at the metal fencing of his kennel, begging for attention. "I'll be right there, boy." His gaze scoured the cramped area again. "I need money to expand and move everything out to the farm."

"Keep praying. It'll happen. We'll get the

grant money and more private funding. You'll see." Meredith picked up Pudding Cup and squeezed her gently. "Oh, there's one other thing." By the hesitant smile registered on her lips, Ethan knew he wasn't going to like the next words out of his cousin's mouth. "We're also getting a ferret. Seems like one of the dogs arriving Saturday thinks it's her baby. I told Private Smith it would be okay."

"But we agreed this would be strictly dogs. It's called Beyond the Borders Dog Sanctuary."

Meredith crossed her arms over her chest and stared at him darkly. "Then change it to Beyond the Borders Animal Sanctuary. As a member of the board, I have the right to speak up, as well. How can you break up a family? What kind of peace of mind would our soldier get if he didn't know both his pets were safe while he was away? I suspect we'll be getting calls for cats soon, too."

Ethan shoved his hand through his hair. "No. Absolutely not. No cats."

"We'll see about that." She gave him a dark look. "Just because you have a personal issue with the cute, cuddly creatures doesn't mean they shouldn't have the same consideration as dogs. They are all God's creatures."

"I'm well aware of that. I'm okay with cats. I just don't understand them. They need to go elsewhere. I'm having enough trouble raising the money and supplies for dogs." His cousin's scowl grew. Half Irish with red hair to match, Meredith was a force to be reckoned with when she was angry. "I'm not going to win this argument, am I?"

She shook her head. "They make medicine for that, you know. I'll make a cat lover out of you yet. I've gotta run, but I'll be back after dinner to help you walk them and transition Bear and Sadie for the night. You really need to get some volunteers in here, though, when the other dogs arrive."

"I'll work on it." Another item to add to his list of things to do for the shelter that grew longer, not shorter, with each passing day. And now to complicate things, he had a whole separate issue to think about.

Holly Stanwyck refused to budge from his mind.

Shadows from the early-morning sun stretched across the road in front of them as Holly drove to the other side of town Saturday morning. The digital clock in her car read 7:57 a.m. and she still had ten minutes to go according to Ethan's directions. Holly disliked being late. The scheduled 7:45 departure time shouldn't have been an issue, since she was an early riser. Too bad her son had other ideas. Holly had let him sleep as long as possible, but he still looked wiped out from the week, disgruntled and a bit dejected. He'd given her a hard time about getting up.

Instead of going to the early church service tomorrow, they'd catch the later one. Not that she really wanted to go, but she had to, for Cam's sake. It hadn't worked these past few months, but maybe being in the Lord's house would straighten him out since she hadn't been able to get through to him. She glanced sideways at her son and caught the scowl underneath the perfected look of boredom. Nothing seemed to have remained from his childhood, and her heart ached at the thought of how things used to be before Jared died.

So much had changed since the accident. Especially the past year.

Holly tried to lighten the mood inside her old Honda. "Mindy's manning the shop today." The high-school student worked for her part-time because Holly couldn't work seven days a week, keep sane and keep Cameron out of trouble, which apparently wasn't working very well. She couldn't really afford the student, but Holly hated asking her friends to continually pitch in. "I need to stop in and check on a few things, but any ideas on what you'd like to do after we finish at Mr. Pellegrino's house?"

"I wanna ride the quad again." He folded his arms across his chest and glared at her.

"You know we don't have them anymore." To help pay their medical bills, she'd sold both ATVs after Jared died.

"That's what I want to do. Patrick tells me they have two. You can let me go home with him after we're finished."

"You know that's not going to happen. Besides, we don't even know if they're coming today to help. They never responded to my phone call." Her fingers gripped the steering wheel a little harder as she turned the corner and merged with the rest of the local and tourist vehicles heading through the downtown area. She couldn't imagine not communicating with another parent had the roles been reversed. But then again, she had no idea what was going on inside Patrick's home, and she had never met his parents.

Silence accompanied them the last five minutes to Ethan's house, where he waited for them outside by the garage with a can of paint and painting supplies. Arms crossed, he paced the small cement area in front of the 1960s-style single-story brick ranch house.

"Good morning." Holly spoke as soon as she

exited the car. Too bad her inability to get her bearings had nothing to do with the sudden movement and everything to do with the man in the old T-shirt underneath his worn camouflage jacket and faded jeans. He still wore the same compassionate look he'd had inside her shop the other day, but underneath she sensed his uncertainty and awkwardness that probably stemmed from his injury in Afghanistan.

"Good morning." His gaze swept over her fleece-lined jacket and then back to her face, making her feel a bit self-conscious. A half smile broke the tension. "I'm glad you're here."

Heat consumed her cheeks. "Sorry we're late. I should have called. I would never back out on a promise or commitment. We just had a hard time getting out of the house this morning." She glanced around the driveway, not surprised to see her car the sole vehicle. "I take it Patrick isn't here?"

"Not yet."

"Then he probably won't show. I was only able to leave a message for his parents, and they never called back." Sorrow and a touch of anger burrowed into her heart. From what she'd gleaned from Cam's conversation the night of the incident, the idea had been Patrick's and so had the spray paint, but her son was just as guilty for going along with the plan.

"That's not your problem. I should have contacted them myself. Ready? After Cameron removes the graffiti, it shouldn't take that long to paint, but we may have to do two coats. We should be finished by eleven. If you need to leave earlier, I can drop Cameron off at the store."

"We? I thought this was Cameron's job."

"It is." Ethan rubbed his chin with the back of his hand, drawing her gaze along with it. "But I somehow feel responsible. If my cousin hadn't mentioned my hastily spoken words—about evicting the tenant because of the back rent—to her best friend, the busybody of Dynamite Creek, your son wouldn't have heard it from his classmate."

She looked at the black spray paint on the light brown wooden door. Holly nodded. "I see. Look, I understand your position. You need someone in there who can pay the rent, and being behind usually results in eviction. I get that. Now, as for the door, you're right, it would go much quicker if we all helped, especially because you haven't seen Cam paint yet." She glanced back at her car. Her son still sat hunched in the front seat. "Today, Cameron. The sooner you get started, the sooner you get finished."

Cam sulked as he stepped from the passenger seat and shuffled toward them. The preteen residing in his body screamed attitude. Holly needed to get a handle on him before he towered above her with his next growth spurt.

Ethan gave Cameron a pair of black work gloves. "Here, put these on."

"For painting?"

"You're going to remove the spray paint first. I doubt the paint for the garage door will cover the black markings very well." After kneeling down, Ethan wedged the yellow bottle with red lettering into the crook of his arm and used his good hand to open the top.

"What's that?" Cameron yanked on the gloves.

"It's supposed to remove the graffiti." Ethan poured some liquid onto a rag, set the bottle down, stood and then handed the cloth to Cam. "Just start rubbing the painted areas. It should come off."

"Me?"

"Of course." He winked at Holly, making her heart flutter until she tamped down on the emotion. Despite the two years that had passed since his death, her heart belonged to Jared.

"You're the one who did it. I'm here to supervise, not do the job for you. Your mom, either. Just be careful you don't get it on your skin or clothes." Folding his arms over his chest, Ethan stepped back.

What? she mouthed, raising her eyebrows and tilting her head to the side. Ethan put a finger to his lips and motioned for her to take a few steps back.

Once they were out of hearing distance, he leaned close to her ear, the warmth of his breath creating havoc with her breathing. "We'll help with the painting. This part is a lesson the boy needs to learn for himself."

"Sounds like you have experience," Holly replied softly as she inched away, needing to distance herself.

"I do. I wasn't exactly a choirboy in my youth." A fraction of a smile tugged at his lips, and his gaze slipped back to her son begrudgingly rubbing the saturated cloth over the paint.

"Really. What did you do?"

"Pretty much the same thing. I tagged a neighbor's garage door because he was old and crotchety. Back then, I didn't get to use any sort of remover. I had to sand the area first, apply a primer and then four coats of paint. Took nearly the whole weekend."

"Did you learn your lesson?"

"That was just one of many."

And yet it looked as if Ethan had managed to turn his life around, go into the service and almost die for his country. Her gaze flickered to his injured hand again and wondered if it still hurt and how he managed to do the day-to-day stuff that required two sets of fingers, but she was too polite to ask. Besides, that would mean opening up her heart again to the possibilities of establishing some sort of friendship or relationship with him, and that wasn't going to happen anytime soon.

"This stuff smells like your nail-polish remover, Mom, but it really works. Look. The paint is almost all gone." Cam broke into her thoughts, dragging them back to the garage door. A slight stain still clung to the beige paint, but it was much less noticeable now. She breathed a sigh of relief, realizing they wouldn't be there all day as she'd anticipated.

"Pretty much. Now you need to rinse the residue off. Then while it's drying I'll show you around."

"Show us around?" Cam dropped the cloth on the newspaper protecting the driveway and yanked off the gloves.

"I'm opening a sanctuary for dogs while their owners are overseas."

"Dogs? Really? I wish we had a dog, not a stupid, silly cat."

Holly heard the criticism and hurt spew from Cam's lips. Her mouth opened and shut quickly as the blood now drained from her cheeks. Any words she could even think to say caught in her throat as she stared at her son and gulped for air. The person standing next to Ethan bore little resemblance to the sweet, innocent boy she remembered.

"Your dad brought Figaro home." That was all Holly managed to say. Pain ate through her heart again, and tears hovered behind her eyelids. How could she explain to her son that the cat was more than just a cat? Figaro was another link to the past she'd shared with Jared, just as Cam was.

Ethan broke the uneasy silence. "Cats are wonderful creatures and just one of God's many creations, Cameron. Pets come in all shapes, sizes and colors. The same as people. God made us all unique. He loves us all the same, despite our differences."

Holly squirmed at Ethan's mention of God. Of course, she should expect no less from a chaplain's assistant, but it made her uncomfortable, especially since she went through the motions for Cam's sake but didn't really believe or love the way she was supposed to.

"I want a dog that can play fetch."

Ethan caught the defiant look the boy threw at his mother, and a subtle change hovered in the air between them. Clouds drifted in front of the sun, blocking out its temporary warmth, and the wind kicked up a notch, intensifying the clang of the wind chime on the front porch of his neighbor's house. Holly's soft gasp met his ears as her light floral fragrance drifted under his nose. Her stricken expression told him more than any words she could speak. The tagging incident aside, the boy was headed for trouble if there wasn't some kind of intervention.

He liked kids, had a special rapport with them. He'd started training as a lay minister after he joined the military, where he had high hopes of saving the world. He hadn't. Instead, five people had paid the ultimate price. But this wasn't about him, the pastor or the two soldiers and civilians with God now. Saving the entire world was His job. Opening the dog sanctuary and maybe helping a troubled boy find the right path in life was something Ethan could handle. Maybe. It was the least he could do for Jared. For Holly.

A thought struck him as he turned on the spigot, yanked the hose to the garage door and then passed it off to Cameron. Ethan knew he should check with Holly first, but he had only so much time to get through to the boy. "I have a solution."

"What?" Both she and Cameron spoke at the same time.

"I need a volunteer or two to work at the dog sanctuary. Cameron can come after school. He'll stay out of trouble, I'll get some much-needed help and the dogs will have someone to play with. He could ride the bus here after school. What do you think?"

"Really?"

"Really. Why play with one dog when you can play with several?" Encouraged by the hope blazing in the boy's eyes, Ethan shot a look at Holly and saw her cross her arms and draw her lips tight.

"Can I, Mom?"

"What about his homework?"

Ethan understood this was about more than just homework. She'd already lost her husband; this was about her son's safety. Despite his being her landlord, she didn't know him from any other stranger in town. He'd reassure her while Cameron rinsed off the door.

A strand of hair had fallen free from her ponytail and accentuated the curve of her jaw-line. Her soft lips graced him with a tentative smile, and her green eyes made him think of his childhood and rolling in cool, thick grass on a hot summer day. Ethan almost forgot why he stood in front of his garage. Almost. He pulled his gaze from her and refocused back on the boy and safer territory. Something about Holly brought out his protective side that, despite what had happened in Afghanistan, was a part of him that refused to go away. And that extended to her son, too.

"I'll make sure he gets his homework done."

"And how will he get home afterward?"

"I'll drive him there."

"I don't know..." Holly felt the weight of two pairs of eyes staring at her. This twist threw another item she had to deal with into her already-crowded mind. Pressure simmered underneath the surface.

"Please, Mom?" Cam begged her.

"Rinse off the door and give me a moment."

Holly should have realized her son wanted a dog. She did know that she couldn't handle the added expense or the time commitment, although the idea of helping out at the shelter was brilliant. Had her monetary worries removed her that far from her son's life? Had she been so focused on getting through each day that she had lost touch with what was the most important to her?

Yes.

Holly didn't like the answer that popped into her head. She didn't understand her son anymore. Jared would have told her to take her troubles to the Lord. Easier said than done.

Holly blamed Him for taking her husband away from her.

Cameron quickly squirted the water onto the door and washed away the paint residue and chemicals. Then he handed the hose back to Ethan. "I'll get my homework done. I won't get into any trouble and I won't ask for a dog again. Please?"

Put like that, how could she say no? Easily. Her alternatives, though, were wondering how to keep Cameron away from Patrick or dealing with her son's sulking expression in the store after school. It would make him happy, settle the issue of Patrick and help Ethan out at the same time. In a way, she owed it to her landlord for letting her stay in the shop until after Christmas.

She still had to deal with the fact that she didn't even know Ethan that well. But he had to be good. He was a Christian, retired from the military and had once been Jared's friend. Plus he was Nan Emrey's son, and she'd never had any issues or concerns with the older woman. Her gut told her it would be okay, but it wouldn't hurt to ask around about him tomorrow just in case. She could always change her mind if necessary.

"Fine. We'll try it out for a week. I'll pick him up, though, after I close the shop. Now shake on the deal and…" Holly turned to face Ethan, the last of her words garbled in her throat. Blood pooled in her cheeks.

This time Ethan had no problem putting out his hand as if almost daring Cameron to touch it.

"What happened to you, Mr. Pellegrino?" Cameron's eyes widened as he stared at Ethan's hand. His own hovered in the space around his head.

A muffled silence filled the space until Holly's strangled voice cut into it. "Cameron. Where are your manners?" Yet she'd asked the same question days earlier.

"Does it hurt?"

"Cameron Jared Stanwyck. Enough." Holly clenched her fists.

Ethan ignored her outburst and leaned toward her son. "Not so much anymore, but when the cold seeps in, it does bother me somewhat."

Flexing his thumb, the only remaining digit on his hand, Ethan stretched it toward Cameron. "Go ahead. You can touch it." He gave her a no-nonsense expression. "I've found talking about it instead of ignoring it helps."

When his gaze caught hers, Holly had a hard time remembering her name. His startling blue eyes had turned into deep, mysterious pools of uncharted waters, challenging her. She fought to gain control over her emotions. What was happening to her?

"Feels weird. How do you write and stuff like that?"

Holly's gaze remained averted, but she sensed Ethan's attention shift to her son. "I'm relearning that, or I do it with my left hand. It hasn't been easy, but I've discovered you can teach an old dog a new trick. Speaking of which, come on. I bet Bear is just waiting to learn something new today."

"Bear?"

"A black Lab that's going to be here for at least a year. He loves to play fetch with an old tennis ball. The temporary sanctuary's in the house until I can move it to the family farm outside of town."

When Cam ran ahead of them, Ethan faced Holly again and held out his injured hand. "Here. Your turn. We may as well get this out of the way, since I'm guessing I'll be seeing a lot of you when you pick Cameron up."

Seeing each other? Holly had no plans on that. She would make sure that Cameron waited for her outside.

"Holly?"

Blinking, she forced her thoughts back to the present. She inhaled sharply. She'd tried to keep from staring earlier, but her gaze had kept returning to his injured hand. She was curious. But to touch it?

Swallowing, Holly reached out. She stopped short. It seemed too intimate a gesture for someone she hardly knew, despite the fact Ethan and Jared had gone to school together. "I'm really not comfortable with this."

"And I'm not going to be comfortable with the idea of seeing the questions in your eyes all the time."

"But—"

"It looks worse than it really is, but I understand." Ethan shrugged and stared at his hand as he withdrew. "It does take getting used to."

"I'm sorry, Ethan."

Holly felt his pain again behind his mask of indifference, confirming there was more going on inside him than he let on. The bomb had taken more than just his fingers and five lives. It left behind a shell of a man, struggling to deal with everyday life. He suffered the survivor's guilt that ate away at the soul like a moth devoured clothing.

Holly wore it every day like a piece of her wardrobe.

She should have never insisted that she and Jared attend the Chamber of Commerce function when the weather forecaster had predicted the cold snap that would turn the melted snow into ice. But how was she to know in that brief moment she took her eyes from the road that the argument would be their last?

Chapter Three

Disappointment pooled around Ethan's shoulders as silence accompanied them to where Cameron stood impatiently by the back door. Holly's son had taken Ethan's injured hand in stride with the curiosity he'd expect from a child. Holly's reaction bothered him, even though it shouldn't. He didn't see the revulsion in her eyes like he had with others, but even now he noticed that her feet angled away from him and she stepped in close proximity to Cameron.

Why had he insisted she touch his hand? Why had he openly challenged her? What difference would it make in the scheme of things? She was his tenant for now, and in less than two months that would change. Then, of course, there was Cameron. But who knew whether that arrangement would last more than a week? More discontent filled him as he stared at the nubs. He didn't understand his actions himself, but he couldn't go back and change things.

If he could, the injury and loss of life would have never happened.

Let go, let God. The voice of the pastor who'd visited him daily in the hospital echoed in his brain. Four simple words; three if you didn't count the repeated one. Was it really that easy? He'd studied God's word, yet he found himself struggling to follow His commands. *Let go, let God.*

Ethan had no choice. In order to embrace the future, the past had to be forgiven and forgotten. Starting today.

"Come on in." He opened the back door and ushered them inside. Warmth spilled around them, along with the scent of lemon, antiseptic and dog. He heard a happy whine as he flipped the light switch, evicting the dimness from the west-facing room.

Nudging the door shut with his shoulder, he glanced around the small white kitchen, realizing the only color came from Holly's red sweatshirt. Nothing adorned the walls but a small black-and-white clock. Even the white curtains on the window over the sink blended into the background, as did the few appliances on the equally white Formica counter.

He'd packed up all his stuff and rented out the

house while he was overseas, and hadn't made the time to unpack the boxes he'd pulled from storage and left in the garage. His house was just a house and not the home he'd left behind. But then again a lot of things had changed. He'd changed. Used to the constant company of people around him for the past several years, the quietness of his surroundings now, other than the two dogs, grated on his nerves.

He'd find the time today to breathe life back into his house.

Another whine sounded from the other room, louder this time since Bear had heard their voices. This time Sadie joined in along with the noise of the chain-link fence rattling as the dogs tried to escape their enclosures.

"Are they this way?" Excitement buried the indifference in Cameron's voice. Good. The boy hadn't gone too far down the wrong path yet. He could work with the spray-paint incident and the few other problems that simmered under the surface.

Maybe this was part of the Lord's plan for Ethan, as well. He'd had an old neighbor's intervention in his teens that helped steer him in the right direction. Now it was time for him to pay it back, not only with Cameron but with other boys, as well—Patrick being one of them if he ever showed up.

"Right through that doorway. Hang on, though. Let me get you some treats for them." Ethan grabbed a box from the pantry, pulled out two bone-shaped dog snacks and then handed them to Cameron. Anticipation created a tangible energy inside the small kitchen, and he knew he'd made the right decision to have the boy help him with the dogs. Holly's signature light floral fragrance mingled with the other scents lingering in the air. He wouldn't turn down her assistance, either, if she decided she wanted to help in some capacity.

"Thanks, Mr. Pellegrino."

It felt right to have Holly and her son inside his home. They added warmth and companionship that were missing between the four walls. Possessions didn't make a home. People did. But allowing others into his life again besides his immediate family meant protecting them. Bile burned his throat and he flexed his throbbing hand, feeling the impression of fingers where none remained. Protecting people was something he wasn't good at anymore. So why the offer to have Cameron help him out?

Because right now, the need to think about the boy's well-being overruled everything else.

"You're welcome. This way. They're in the Arizona room." Ethan slipped past his guests and into the area to his left that used to be the back porch before the previous owner enclosed it. Six kennels filled the space, all lined up like soldiers during inspection.

But this was only temporary. As soon as he found more funding, he'd be moving to the permanent sanctuary outside of town. The vision of twenty-four more inside the old barn on the farm property filled his mind's eye as well as the big dog run in the pasture.

Focus on the future.

Cameron shook off his mother's grasp and ran to the first kennel. A smile broke out as he put his hand out for the black Lab to smell. Good. The kid knew how to approach a dog. And he showed an interest in them and an apparent love for them as he reached through the bars and scratched the dog behind his ears. That would make their time together go a bit smoother.

He glanced at Holly and momentarily lost himself in her presence. With her hair pulled back in a ponytail and no makeup to cover her smooth, delicate skin, she looked to be in her mid-twenties even though he figured her to be closer to his thirty-five years. The swept-back locks exposed her long, elegant neck and, from this angle, a straight, slightly upturned nose. But it was her vulnerability that got to him.

Despite her attempts to keep it all together, he

sensed just below the surface she suffered and struggled with her son, the shop, everyday life. Ethan also knew he hadn't made it any easier on her, but he had his own dreams and issues. His gaze fell on his hand. Sometimes sugarcoating things didn't help; it only made matters worse. He'd given her to the end of the year, and his offer to help her son would still be available to both of them as long as the arrangement continued to work out.

He should step away and draw himself inward. Instead, when she turned her head toward him, he found himself staring into her deep green eyes that had seen so much pain. A pain he could identify with. He'd lost his father at a young age, and several of his friends in Afghanistan. He could identify with the hollowness, the gaping hole, the huge cavity filled with darkness that even these days God's light had a hard time driving away. But even that couldn't compare to losing one's partner, one's soul mate.

He had no experience with that sort of loss, yet he felt the need to comfort. Protect. He wanted to draw Holly into his arms, absorb her pain and blend it with his own.

"What's his name?"

Ethan blinked at Cameron's words, stepped backward and concentrated on the dog as Holly knelt down by her son. He folded his arms across his chest and leaned against the door frame. "That's Bear. He'll be with me for at least a year. He likes to play ball. I've already taken him out for a walk, but in between the coats of paint, maybe you can let him run around the yard a bit and throw him a couple of balls."

"Hi, Bear." Laughter spilled from the boy's lips as the dog tried to lick his face through the metal fencing. In that instant, Ethan realized another thing that had been missing from his life. Not that he'd had anything to laugh about. That would change going forward. He flexed what remained of his right hand again, determined not to let anything stop him from his goals.

And maybe find love in the process.

A strange emotion gripped Ethan as he squatted down beside Holly outside the kennel of the cocker spaniel/heeler mix next to Bear. The tan-and-white spotted dog with the droopy ears stared up at them with big brown eyes. Love? Something as complicated as that was meant for guys like her late husband, not someone who would probably have nightmares of what happened in Afghanistan for the rest of his life, or carry the guilt of five deaths around his neck like a yoke.

"This one here is Sadie. She'll be here for almost two years." God willing he'd still be open then. More delays in funding meant he would have to pull more money out of his savings account to continue the renovations, because with more dogs coming in, he had to have more room.

"She's adorable," Holly whispered. He noticed her gaze dart toward Cameron, who had wedged his hand between the metal bars of the cage door and continued to scratch Bear behind his ears. "Maybe I should consider getting Cam a dog. In the future." Her sigh washed over him, filling him with that need to protect her from her thoughts. Ironically, he was part of the problem, not the solution, since her reprieve lasted until just after the holidays.

"Where are the rest of the dogs?" Cameron asked.

"Two dogs are showing up this afternoon and the other two arrive next week."

"What happens if you get another dog? There won't be any room." Holly turned to face him.

"I'm well aware of that. I'll have plenty of room once I move to the permanent place."

"But in order to move there, you need money. Like the rent from the storefront." Holly dipped her head and clenched her fists. But when she made eye contact with him again, resolve and resignation slid into her eyes. "What you're doing is a noble thing, Ethan. I'll vacate immediately so you can get another renter in there."

"It's going to take a lot more than those kinds of funds. The past-due rent isn't going to make that much of a difference. My original offer still stands. You have until December 31."

For a moment Ethan stared at the empty kennels and again envisioned himself in his new place with twenty-four kennels occupied and his sanctuary fully operational. Somehow he sensed the woman who barely grazed his shoulder and the boy kneeling in front of the other kennel would play an intricate role in this if he managed to pull it off.

The Lord worked in mysterious ways.

"Come on, the door should be dry by now. Let's put the primer on and then we'll come back and take the dogs outside for a bit."

"Aw, just a few more minutes?" Cameron whined.

"We'll come back." Ethan held his ground. The integral part of the intervention was taking a firm hand and making sure the preteen knew who was boss.

Fifteen minutes later, they all stepped back and looked at their handiwork. Holly grinned and scratched the back of her neck. "Now I know why I leave the painting to the professionals. Your area looks much better than mine."

"And mine." Cameron plopped his brush back into the paint tray.

"It's primer. It won't matter, anyway. Not once the topcoat goes on. I'll show you a quick, easy way to do it when we get to that step."

"It's a good thing you placed cardboard along the bottom. It saved the concrete driveway from the wayward drops."

"Yeah, it's a lesson learned the hard way." Ethan grabbed the brushes and rollers to rinse off with the hose. "If you study the driveway enough, you'll see the drops of paint from the first time I painted it six years ago when I bought the house. No matter how careful you are, you always make mistakes."

Funny. He could forgive himself for certain mistakes, but not others. But then again, a little paint on the concrete couldn't even compare to five people losing their lives because he was distracted. Careless.

If only he could wash away his guilt as quickly as he did the primer. The stream of water cleared. After shutting off the tap, he stood and shook everything out. "Good job, Cameron. We'll make a painter out of you yet. There'll be lots of painting needed in the new offices of the sanctuary. What do you say? Wanna come on board?"

"Sounds like too much work. Can I go back and play with Bear now?"

Ethan couldn't help but smile. At least the kid was honest. Cameron would probably rather go to the dentist than do any more painting, but at least he had energy for the dogs. Exercising the dogs took a lot of time, time Ethan could use for paperwork, or raising money, or cleaning up the kennels, if he didn't make that part of Cameron's responsibilities. "Just make sure you put him on the leash hanging on the wall before you take him outside."

"Sure thing. Thanks, Mr. Pellegrino." Cameron spun around and sprinted away, leaving Holly and Ethan to follow at a more leisurely pace.

"It's sunny today, so it should dry quickly. Then we can do a coat of paint. If that doesn't cover it, I'll do another one tomorrow."

"Tomorrow? But I thought we'd get it all done today."

He watched Holly swipe her fingers across her old sweatshirt, leaving gray streaks of primer in the process. That and the tiny splotches sprinkling her hair only added to her charm. It was all he could do not to try to remove some of the bigger blotches, but after his earlier thoughts about her surfaced, he knew that it wasn't a good idea. Instead, he focused on Cameron.

"That had been my plan, but keeping you here all day wasn't part of it, either. I forgot about factoring in the time frame of letting the coats dry in between applications. Cameron will have fulfilled his obligation after the first coat of paint."

"But—"

"If I do another coat, that is my own choice, okay? You have enough going on. Let's just keep it at that."

Holly reflected on his words. He understood, and that scared her more than the thought of losing the shop. Because if she ever decided to let go of what she had with Jared and started dating again, Ethan would be the kind of man she'd choose to go out with. But she wouldn't. Involvement with another man would only open herself up to more heartache and pain, especially if something happened to him. Besides, she needed to concentrate on her son and his needs. Once he was grown, she could focus on her own.

"I haven't seen Cameron this excited in a long time." *Since before Jared's death.* "Thanks for giving him the chance. I'm sure he'll do a great job with the dogs. And I doubt he'll give you any trouble with his homework if he's got something to look forward to afterward."

"He doesn't like doing his homework?"

"Not lately. Or pick up after himself, or do any of his chores." Her sigh filled the space between them. "There's a lot of things he used to like to do but not anymore. His attitude these past few months has been...for lack of a better word...challenging."

Holly had to get a grip on it, or the spray-paint incident at Ethan's was only the beginning. Some days she didn't know where to turn. Jared would have told her to look upward and let everything rest in God's hands. Yet He hadn't answered her prayers to keep her husband alive. What made her think He'd listen to her now?

"I've worked with kids before. I'll see if I can get through to him."

He put his hand into his pocket but pulled it out empty. A pained expression flickered across his face, quickly restrained and replaced by one of resignation.

"Is something wrong? Did you hurt yourself?" She placed her hand on his forearm and compassion infused her. Only a bit lower and she could touch his hand. His injured hand. Did she want to go there? Only confusion answered her.

"No. I'm okay. I used to always have candy for the Afghan children. Sometimes I forget where I am. I don't carry it anymore."

"I'm sorry."

Ethan moved her hand from his arm and squeezed it gently before he let it drop. "What's there to be sorry for? For some reason God spared me but left me a reminder that He's in charge. Despite my teachings in order to be a lay minister and everything I've witnessed, I forget."

Unsure of what to say next, Holly trudged along beside him the rest of the way to the back of the house in silence. What could she say that wouldn't sound phony or unbelievable?

Holly paused in the parking lot of the shingled one-story redbrick building. Despite her almost weekly attendance, she still felt uncomfortable since her husband's death. This had been Jared's church, his parents' church and his grandparents' church before him in the old building that now housed the youth center and other Sunday school classes. It was as if they knew she didn't have the same beliefs, that she'd shut down her connection with God the same time He'd taken Jared away. Some days she felt the eyes of the congregation staring at her, drilling her as she sat in one of the back rows, as if they blamed her for her husband's death.

That wasn't too far from the truth.

Beside her, Cam shifted in his seat and refused to take off his seat belt. "Do we really have to go?"

"Yes, we really have to go. I let you sleep in, so you're stuck with the traditional service today. Come on, we'll go grab brunch after we're done." Not that she could afford it, but both of them needed some sort of treat. The Sunrise Diner wasn't too far from the store, and it catered to the folks who didn't have a lot of money to spend, unlike the more touristy places on the square.

Afterward, she'd drop her son off at his friend Tyler's house while she opened the store for a few hours since Mindy wasn't feeling well today. If the sunny weather held, the afternoon should be somewhat busy and she could reduce her inventory by making a bunch of sales. That would be less for her and Cameron to pack after Christmas.

If they even had a Christmas. So far she'd had no response to her seasonal decorating flyer, but it was still early in the season. She'd thought her idea had been a good one. Apparently, it wasn't.

The butterflies in her stomach increased with each step. She joined the streams of other worshippers entering the church, yet Holly still felt the isolation despite the beige welcome mat by the door. It was probably more of her own doing than anyone milling around her, though.

She and Cam wandered inside, stopping only to pick up a bulletin on their way through the door and into the interior. Grabbing one of the last open pews on the left side of the aisle, Holly sank down and stared at the tall white candles that graced the two candleholders on each side of the pulpit. Christine Preston, one of the store owners on her side of the street, made them, along with some of the other candles in other areas of the church.

Mrs. O'Leary, in her usual bright, tropical attire, sat behind the organ to her right, the pull of the music impossible to ignore. On each side of the building, three large, narrow windows allowed sunlight to stream in, casting a kaleidoscope of color on the stairs leading up to the altar.

Too bad her mood didn't match the tranquil setting. Especially when Ethan stepped through the double doors and sat down on the pew next to Cam. "Good morning."

"Morning." Of the few open seats left in the sanctuary, why did he choose to sit with them? As a local, he had to know a lot of people inside. But when he tilted his head and spoke into her son's ear, her heart fluttered at the sight of her son's grin. Whatever Ethan told him had adjusted his attitude. For the time being, anyway.

And here Holly thought the man would only

help during the hours Cam was at the dog sanctuary. Apparently, she'd been wrong. She flashed him a smile, but sitting with him, despite her widow status, would have the tongues of the town gossips wagging. The last thing she needed was another rumor getting back to Cam, even if there was no truth to this one. Her son had taken her closing the shop after the holidays well, but he had yet to think about the alternative of how she was going to earn money. Or if he had, he hadn't mentioned a word to her.

But Holly thought about it constantly, even when she should be concentrating on the service. Moisture gathered on her palms as she dug into her purse to retrieve her paltry offering. Despite her problems right now, there were people worse off than her. She still had a roof over her and her son's heads and could still put some food on the table.

"So who's ready for Thanksgiving?" Pastor Matt rubbed his stomach and glanced at the front row, where his wife and two teenage boys sat.

The congregation laughed. Everyone knew the pastor appreciated food. They were barely into the start of November, but Holly had been more focused on Christmas than anything else. Like last year, she'd bring a pumpkin pie and loaf of homemade bread to her friend Kristen's house for the big meal.

"So in that spirit of Thanksgiving, along with the offering you've just given, I'd like to take some time to reflect on the meaning of a stuffed turkey, gravy and mashed potatoes by reading you the passage Thessalonians 5:16–18. 'Be joyful always; pray continually; give thanks in all circumstances, for this is God's will for you in Christ Jesus.' Notice it says 'in all.' And we know that God is there with us to help us through it all. And for that we have to be thankful.'"

Holly suddenly realized she was thankful for more than she thought. She had her house, her son and her friends. Her gaze drifted over Cam's head to where Ethan sat. Could she include him in her circle? Her cheeks warmed at the thought, especially when his lips turned up at the corners as he glanced her way.

"Now, during this time of thanksgiving, we start to think about our wants and needs." Pastor Matt continued, and Holly faced forward, determined to listen to every word the pastor spoke, instead of dwelling on the man who might be able to help her with her son. "Not that there is anything wrong with that, but sometimes we don't go to the right place to get those needs met. Do you turn to friends? Family? Significant others? Shouldn't you be turning to the Lord first?"

Maybe that was Holly's problem.

Instead of blaming the Lord for taking Jared from her because there was nothing that could be done about it now, she should be turning to Him to help her sort things out. Let Him help her with her needs instead of trying to figure everything out. Maybe that was why Ethan had been brought into her life. Still, letting go of the past and moving forward challenged her way of thinking and wasn't going to happen overnight, despite Pastor Matt's comforting words.

"Great sermon today, Pastor Matt." Ethan stepped into the refreshment line behind the man with the receding hairline that had started to gray at the temples.

"Did it help you?" Matt looked at him compassionately. "So often I think I'm not getting through to the congregation."

"It did." Ethan clutched his hands. He'd prayed along with everyone else that by letting God attend to his needs he'd be able to better deal with everyone else with more compassion, mercifulness and forgiveness, Holly and Cameron included.

"Good." Matt patted him on the back before he grabbed a plate. "Now I can enjoy my snack knowing I've done my job with at least one of my flock. Was there something else you wanted to discuss? Like how you can better participate in your church family?"

Ethan knew this was coming. Every week since his return, the pastor had brought up the subject. This time, though, he was prepared. "In a way. I have a new raffle item for the Charity Ball next weekend."

"Good. We're always on the lookout for more stuff. What is it?"

"Holly Stanwyck is starting a seasonal decorating business. She'd like to raffle off her services." Ethan glanced over his shoulder, looking for his tenant. He hadn't exactly told her earlier that this was the idea that he had for increasing her new business, but if she left a stack of cards out with the raffle item, it was another way for her to get her name out there. Of course, he probably should have checked with her first. Now he had to tell her just what he'd volunteered her for.

Since it was his idea, he'd go along and help with the project as best he could. He had no decorating sense, but he could follow directions. If all worked well, maybe some of her skills would rub off on him when it came to accessorizing the office and waiting area for his new sanctuary.

"That's great. Get me her donation information so I can put it out with the other items before this weekend."

When Holly came into view with Cameron in tow, Ethan excused himself. "I'll get one of her flyers and deliver it tomorrow."

"One more thing before you go. Have you thought about helping out with the Youth Ministry?"

Ethan rubbed his good hand along the back of his neck. His gaze darted to Cameron before he made eye contact with Pastor Matt again. "I have. But I think I need to do it on a smaller scale than what you have envisioned, and not just within this church. There's several misguided youth here in town that could use some intervention. I plan on utilizing them at the sanctuary and teaching them God's word, as well."

Pastor Matt clapped him on the back again. "That's a great idea. And I think I have an excellent candidate for you if you haven't discovered him yet."

"Cameron Stanwyck?" Ethan set his plate down on the counter and placed a few pieces of fruit and half a poppy-seed muffin on it.

"That's the one."

Cameron had a reputation. Not good. It looked as if his intervention had come just in time. Ethan's hand shook a bit as he picked up his food. After everything that had happened, was he ready for this? Yes. He'd make sure he had no distractions this time when he supervised Holly's son and any other boy he had out at the farm. He spied her in the thinning crowd. "I thought so. I'll get you that information about Holly's service this week."

Weaving his way through the room, Ethan planted himself next to Holly. "I have something I need to discuss with you. How about some breakfast? These snacks just aren't cutting it."

Cameron grunted his approval.

Too bad Holly couldn't muster up the same enthusiasm.

What could Ethan want to discuss with her? They'd painted the garage yesterday, and Ethan had said not to worry about the second coat, that he'd do it this afternoon on his own.

Maybe he'd changed his mind about letting Cam help him after school? Or could he have found a renter and needed her to vacate immediately?

She fingered the gold cross suspended from her neck when she returned his gaze. Lines furrowed his forehead and his lips zipped into a straight line. Her heart stalled. Whatever he needed to discuss didn't look good as she floundered in the depths of his gaze. It took a few moments for her voice to work properly. "Sure. We were going to the Sunrise Diner for brunch. Would you care to join us?"

Holly twirled her hair around her finger and stared out at the grayness pushing against the glass. The streetlight out front burned through a cone-shaped area of gloom, accentuating the empty sidewalk. Sunday should have been a good day for sales. With just a handful of customers wandering through her front doors, discouragement settled around her shoulders as she cradled the phone to her ear. "I don't know, Kristen, even running a twenty-percent-off sale isn't enough to entice people inside. Maybe I should just blow out all the merchandise and close up as quickly as possible."

"I'm so sorry. I'll keep praying that something changes. I know you've worked so hard to keep Jared's dream alive. Maybe that idea of Ethan's will work? I think it's brilliant that he thought to raffle off your services at the church raffle."

"That would be nice."

"And what's even better is that he's going to help you with it. And he's helping you with Cam. Wouldn't it be great if something else came out of it, too?"

Kristen, the hopeless romantic. Holly wasn't interested in replacing Jared.

"It's starting to snow outside and it's bound to get worse. I've gotta run, Kristen." Holly said goodbye to her best friend, hung up and began shutting off the lights so she could go pick up Cameron.

She hated driving in the snow, especially now. The weather had been worse that night the accident claimed not only Jared but also the life fluttering inside her womb. She still had nightmares about it. If anything happened to Cam, her only link to her late husband, she'd never forgive herself. She still hadn't with Jared and baby Olivia.

Chapter Four

❧

"Hi, Cameron." Ethan met Holly's son at the end of his driveway Monday afternoon. Relief mingled with a bit of trepidation filled him. The boy had shown up, which meant he didn't have to go search for him or make that phone call to Holly, but it was also a big commitment. Sure, he was good with kids, liked them, wanted one or two of his own someday, yet his dealings with those Afghan children had been on a superficial level. This was different in so many ways. Somehow he knew, though, that God meant for him to intervene here. "School go okay today?"

The boy grunted a response, his gaze darting around him as if searching for something. "Where's Bear?"

"Inside with Sadie and the other two that arrived Saturday afternoon. Come on."

"They came. Yes!" Delight lit the boy's expression, and he quivered with excitement.

Ethan had had no doubts that this arrangement would work. Still, the boy's reaction made him happy. A willing student always made things easier, but he was glad he hadn't brought Bear out to meet him, because he didn't want the distraction. "And two more are arriving this week. I'll introduce you to them, but no work until your homework is done."

"Homework?"

"Homework first. That's the agreement I made with your mom."

"That rots."

"Not really. Education is important." Ethan scratched the back of his neck. He'd gone into the military right after high school instead of college like Cameron's father, figuring life training was better than a formal education. He didn't regret his decision, but he'd changed his mind while serving by taking lay ministry courses online when he could and had just enrolled in a few night courses at the local community college to improve his business skills.

A few stray leaves crunched under their feet, and a crow cawed from the towering pine tree on the other side of the driveway as they made their way to the back of Ethan's house. A cool, crisp breeze laden with a hint of the encroaching winter made him snuggle deeper into his warm jacket. Some snow remained from last night's brief storm, and the temperatures had dropped.

Despite his love for his hometown and the numerous family members that remained, he disliked the cold. The winter weather wrapped around his body and seeped into his limbs. He dug his hands farther into his pockets to keep them warm. Opening the sanctuary in Phoenix hadn't been an option because of the extreme heat in the summer. That and the simple fact his mother had leased him the fifty acres of land outside Dynamite Creek that held the old family farmhouse and a barn at a rock-bottom price so he could operate Beyond the Borders Dog Sanctuary. Although right now he missed the warmth of the Valley and the Middle East.

Five minutes later, after the introductions to the newest occupants, Ethan poured a glass of milk and set out some apple slices, peanut butter and crackers. The boy would probably prefer the chocolate-chip cookies, but Ethan didn't want to feed him any unnecessary sugar before he had a chance to discuss what type of diet Holly followed.

"Here's a snack."

Discomfort lodged between his shoulder blades. Was he usurping Holly's role? Maybe a little, but he was also helping her, and that had to outweigh everything. The boy needed this; he needed the help, and the dogs needed the attention.

"So what do you have for homework?"

"Just math."

Ethan didn't buy that. He may not have kids of his own, but he'd already lived through middle school and he probably still knew some of the teachers at Dynamite Creek Middle School. Kids always had homework. Even over school breaks.

"Let's see your agenda."

"You don't trust me?"

"Should I?" He stared Cameron down. The boy held his gaze for a few seconds before he looked away. Ethan recognized that look of being busted; Holly's son had worn it the day he caught him and his friend spray painting the garage.

"No. I have social studies and science, too." Cameron pulled out the binder that held his notebooks and agenda from his backpack.

"No English?"

"It's called language arts now."

"Okay. No language arts homework?"

"No. I did it in class."

This time Ethan sensed the boy was telling the truth. "Good. So who's your language arts teacher this year?"

"Mrs. Metcalf."

He blinked and wrinkled his forehead. "She's still there? She's got to be near retirement now. She was one of my teachers when I went there."

"Really?"

Ethan almost laughed at the raised eyebrows and O-shaped lips. "Yeah, really. Don't look so surprised. I'm about the same age as your mom. If I remember correctly, your dad had Mrs. Metcalf, too."

"You knew my dad?"

"We used to be friends." Ethan squeezed his eyes shut and rubbed his face. An image of a high-school-aged Jared imprinted itself on the inside of his eyelids. He could see his father's influence in Cameron's features, though his blond coloring came from Holly's side. "I'm sorry he passed away, Cameron. I know it's got to be hard on you, eating you alive on the inside while you try to hide it from everyone else."

A scowl replaced the boy's earlier surprise and Ethan felt him pull away. "How would you know?"

The camaraderie they'd shared a few moments ago disappeared, but Ethan knew he had to reach out to the boy or he'd lose him. That wasn't an option. God had brought Cameron into his life for a reason, just as He'd given him the idea about the dog sanctuary. Maybe they were meant to help each other out; the dogs, too.

"I know because my dad passed away when I was just a year older than you were. It hurts. It leaves a hole in your heart and makes you feel like you're floundering in a sea of monsters. You don't know where to turn or who to reach out to. So you beat yourself up, lash out at the world, feel the injustice and want to hurt things, spray-paint things, maybe hurt yourself, too. But nothing changes the fact that he's gone, and you blame yourself."

White pinched the skin around Cameron's mouth, and anger flashed from eyes that looked so much like Holly's that Ethan was taken aback for a moment. Like mother, like son. Holly hadn't recovered from Jared's death, either. When the boy slouched at the table and buried his face in his hands, Ethan recognized the pain. He'd worn it so many times as a youth until it became a second skin. With the help of his old neighbor, though, he'd finally managed to shed it in high school.

"Come on. Get your homework done so you can play with the dogs." Ethan changed the subject and picked up the envelope that had slipped out of Cameron's agenda. Since it had Holly's name on it, he didn't open it, but he doubted it was a report card. "What's this?"

The boy flopped back into his chair, glanced at the envelope and then back down at his notebook.

"I asked you a question, Cameron. I expect and deserve an answer. If you can't have the respect to do that, then I'm not sure how well we'll work together with the dogs."

A stricken look flashed across his features. This time he had no trouble finding words to say. "You mean I can't work here after all?"

"That's a choice you have to make. I want an open form of communication and need to feel that I can trust you. We made a great start. Let's keep it that way."

"It's a letter from my math teacher. I'm not doing good. I mean, I just don't get the stuff we're covering. It all gets so jumbled up in my head."

"Does your mom know?"

Cameron shook his head. "She doesn't get it, either. I mean, she's good with numbers, but all this algebra stuff…"

"What is it?"

"She's just so busy all the time. And worried." Cameron played with his pencil in one hand and twirled his hair through his fingers with the other. "I can't talk to her anymore. Things used to be so different."

Ethan pulled out a chair and sat down. He'd

made a promise to Cameron earlier, and he wouldn't go back on his word. The phone calls and paperwork could wait a few more minutes. "Want to talk about it?"

"Yeah. We used to have so much fun."

"It's hard trying to take care of everything by yourself. Life, just like math, can get pretty overwhelming at times. I'm sure your mom is doing the best she can. How many of these communications have you gotten?"

"First one." Cameron refused to look him in the eye.

"Try again."

"This is my fourth."

"And who signed off on them? Your mom?"

Silence filled the kitchen.

"You signed your mom's name, didn't you?"

Guilt flashed across the boy's features before he hung his head in shame.

Ethan dug his hands through his hair. Holly had more to worry about than she realized. His gaze rose, taking in the stark whiteness of the kitchen ceiling, but he wasn't really paying attention. *Thank you, Lord, for bringing me into Cameron's life.* That the boy needed more guidance was an understatement. He couldn't fault Holly. She'd done a great job so far, but he knew from firsthand experience now that he was opening the sanctuary how much time it took to run a business. She had a son and household to run by herself, as well.

"We're going to have a talk with your mom when she picks you up. Now, I have a few phone calls to make and some paperwork to do. Finish up your other homework and I'll come help you with the math. That actually was one of my best subjects, behind lunch."

"Lunch?"

Ethan tried to lighten the mood swirling around the kitchen. "Yeah. If they gave out grades for that, I would have gotten an A."

Cameron smiled. "You're okay, Mr. Pellegrino."

"Call me Mr. P. if that's easier, or Ethan if your mom approves."

An hour later, Cameron closed his math book and stretched. Ethan did the same. They did things differently now in school with the new programs the administration and government had put in place, but at least the fundamentals were the same. Cameron was a smart kid; he just needed to be shown by example and given an explanation how to do the problems.

Ethan pushed his chair back and stood. "Good work. Now, what else do you know about dogs?"

"They like to be played with?"

"And?"

"They need to be fed and have lots of water?"

"And?" Ethan sensed the boy was toying with him.

"They like to be scratched and petted?"

"All of the above, but you're forgetting one basic thing. They need to be cleaned up after."

"But I thought I was here to play with them."

"That's one reason, but you're also here to help. And that would include making sure that the environment is safe and healthy for them."

"What do I need to do first?"

Ethan threw Cameron his jacket and led him to the back porch, where he handed him a small rake and scooper. "I think you know what to do with these. And after that, their food and water dishes need to be washed out. Then, after you brush them, it'll be time to play."

Knowing that her son was in good hands, Holly had stayed open a bit later than usual to accommodate another decent sale. Her cat wouldn't be too happy with the delayed dinner, but Mrs. Hendricks had come in to buy several ornaments for her book-club ladies along with the remaining snow globes so she could start a family tradition with her new grandbabies. Business had also been good for a Monday and Holly had actually made a profit. If she could sustain it, she'd have a lot less to box up and sell on eBay and actually make more than a minimum payment on her credit cards for once.

Since she knew she'd get home too late to scrounge something together, she stopped at the grocery store to pick up dinner. Holly hadn't asked if Ethan had made any plans, but she'd picked up enough fried chicken and side dishes to feed them all if he didn't mind sharing his kitchen with them for the meal.

Recyclable cloth bags in hand, she stepped quietly from her car, not wanting to disrupt the scene playing out in front of her. Both Ethan and Cameron stood in the backyard, throwing tennis balls to Bear and Sadie. When Ethan placed a hand on her son's shoulder and pointed at something off to their left, the scene brought tears to her eyes. Cameron needed a male influence in his life.

The action made her miss Jared again.

"Hello?" Her voice wobbled. She had to get a grip on herself. Not only for Cam's sake but her own, as well.

"Hi, yourself." Ethan waved, a tentative smile on his lips, his gaze never leaving her face as she approached.

"Mom." Cam ran toward her and flung his arms around her waist. "You're here. Wait till you see what Oreo can do."

"Oreo?" Holly dragged in a breath of cold air

and focused on her son. Her attention should be on him, not the man who sent conflicting emotions through her at a mere glance.

"One of the new dogs. She can catch a disc in her mouth and then bring it back. She's in her kennel now, but we can go get her."

"I can't wait to see it. I brought some dinner." Holly held up the bags. "I figured you guys would be hungry after a full day at work and school. You don't mind, do you, Ethan?"

"'Course not. Eating was his favorite subject," Cam broke in. "Here, let me help you and then you can watch me with Oreo."

The turnaround in her son caught Holly by surprise. She'd hoped Ethan would be a good influence on her son, but over time, not just in a few short hours. Holly took in Ethan's crooked smile and the way the light wind ruffled his wavy dark brown hair. She'd never noticed the slight dimples before, which added another dimension to his character. In her core, she felt a tiny ripple, somehow knowing she could depend on Ethan no matter what.

"Things went okay today?"

"Better than can be expected. There is a small issue with his math he needs to show you, but I think we've got a handle on it now. Other than that, Cameron's a great kid. He's just hitting that tough age to be a boy. Do you have anything else that needs to come inside?"

Holly shook her head and walked beside Ethan as they made their way to his back porch. Math. Ugh. She was glad Ethan had been able to help Cameron because what her son was studying wasn't her strong point. Accounting, yes; algebra, no.

In the kitchen, Holly pulled out the food while Ethan scrambled for plates and utensils. In the background, she could hear Cam talking to the dogs as he put dry food into their bowls. The scene held more promise of a future than Holly was accustomed to. Night had descended beyond the windowpanes, adding a cozier feel to the small kitchen than she was comfortable with. It almost felt like it had before with Jared. Their last meal. Except that time, she had the flutter of life inside her. Dinner hadn't been a good idea, but with everything Ethan was doing for her son, she felt compelled to return some sort of favor. Cam reentered the room, washed his hands and went to sit down.

"Wait a minute." Ethan stopped Cam from sitting at the table. "A gentleman always pulls out the chair for a lady." Ethan moved the chair back and motioned for Holly to sit. The action brought more than a flutter to her pulse.

It brought back a simpler time, when the little things mattered.

Ethan took his seat, bowed his head and clasped his hands together. "Dear Lord, thanks for providing us with the food we are about to receive that comes from all Your good graces. In Jesus's name we say amen."

"Amen." Holly spoke the word, but it held little meaning for her. Would she ever be able to believe again like her late husband had, or the man sitting across from her? She'd tried on numerous occasions and continued to go to church, but she didn't feel it. She'd believed once, but in her sorrow and anger, she'd turned off her belief and tuned Him out. Despite what the Bible said, would God and Jesus welcome her back if she decided to do more than go through the motions? Would They hear her if she really prayed? And did she want to go there?

Each question brought more anxiety, and despite her lack of an appetite, her dinner disappeared in less than ten minutes. Holly's fingers trembled as she wiped her mouth and put her paper napkin on her plate to cover the chicken bones. She had a more immediate concern. "I got a phone call about my decorating business today. My first."

"Congratulations. And don't forget, the holiday raffle at the church is Sunday. You're sure to get more calls after that."

"There's just one problem." Holly almost couldn't get the words out of her mouth. "It's Saturday morning, and I'll probably be gone most of the day. The mayor wants his house decorated for his annual gala that night. Neither he nor his wife is up to it, and their handyman is down with the flu." Or that was what Mayor Moss claimed, but no matter what the excuse or charitable contribution, she couldn't turn it down. Her gaze froze on Cam.

"But, Mom, that's the day of the Fall Harvest Festival at the Community Center. You promised." Disappointment and anger chased away Ethan's progress.

"I know, Cam. We'll go. It might just be later than we expected." Guilt tore at her insides and the tension in the room threatened to suffocate her. They hadn't been to the festival since Jared died, but the decorating job was a big one, and realistically she wondered if she could handle it by herself.

She had to.

The job paid way more than she needed to put out for Mindy to work the shop Saturday as long as she was feeling better. It would help pay down some of her personal bills and put away some money for Christmas. Her gaze froze on

Ethan. Would he expect her to pay some of her back rent with it? Everyone in town knew Mayor Moss came from old money.

Ethan must have read her mind, because he shook his head slightly. "Drop Cameron off here and he can help me with the dogs, especially the new ones arriving Wednesday. Then after we're done here, we'll come help you decorate. I haven't been to a Fall Harvest Festival since I graduated high school. It'll be fun."

"No, Mom. You promised we would go for the entire day. Just you and me." Cameron jumped up and toppled his chair back. White surrounded his tight lips and he visibly shook. "We haven't done anything fun since Dad died. All you do is work, and worry and cry when you don't think I'm looking."

Holly also stood, at a loss on how to deal with her son. She wanted to reach out and hold him, but her hands remained clenched at her sides. She didn't know what to say to him any-more, especially when he spoke the truth. Heat flushed her cheeks at the airing of their family problems. "Cameron. Please. We'll talk about this later."

"That's what you always say and it never happens."

Ethan's chair scraped across the tile floor. The tension in the room set him on edge, bringing his own issues to the forefront. "Stop it, both of you. I have an idea. Come with me."

He motioned for them to follow him into one of the rooms he'd converted into a gym. Beyond the treadmill and just past the weight machine, a punching bag hung from the far ceiling. The psychologist had told him that releasing his anger from what he called "the incident" would help with his emotional recovery. Maybe the same would apply to Cameron. Holly would benefit from it, too.

"You have a workout room?" Anger still rolled off Cameron. "We used to have a membership to the YMCA. I used some of the things in the teen center until my mom didn't renew." He glared at Holly and slapped his hand down on the weight machine.

"You know why I had to do that."

"When are we ever going to have enough money? And now that you're closing the shop, we'll have even less."

"But I'll have the decorating business."

"And even less time for me." The boy's shoulders sagged, his voice now barely a whisper.

Holly welcomed her son into her embrace. She closed her eyes and placed her cheek on top of his head. "Oh, Cam. I'm so sorry."

Ethan knew he'd made the right decision to bring them in here. They both needed to exorcise their anger and memories. He gave them a few moments before he broke the shattered breathing in the room. "This way."

He pointed toward the back corner of the room by the window.

"You have a punching bag?" Cameron broke away from his mother.

"Helps relieve tension and anger. I want you to walk over there and punch it. You, too, Holly."

First Cameron tapped the bag with his fist, then Holly. She shook her hand but then tapped it again. The bag barely moved. He'd expected the boy to do it, but not his mother. His plan might work better than he'd thought.

"That's the best you guys can do?" Ethan stepped in between them and egged them on, trying to re-create the energy in the kitchen. The therapy didn't work unless both Cameron and Holly could release their anger. He'd work on Cameron first.

"No!" Cameron struck the bag again with more force, but not enough to make it sway very far.

"Your dad is dead. How do you feel about that?" Ethan punched the bag himself, feeling the spurt of adrenaline through his veins. He needed his own dose of therapy right now, too.

Cameron punched the bag again, and this

time, Ethan knew he'd hit it as hard as he could by his grunt. "It rots."

"You know what else rots?" Ethan didn't wait for the boy to respond as he punched the bag again. "What rots is that I don't have any fingers anymore on my right hand. What are you angry at, Holly?"

For a few heartbeats, Holly just stood there and stared at the bag. Anger, hurt and denial all took up residence on her face and in her stance. For a moment, Ethan didn't think she'd go along with his plan until he saw the resignation disappear behind determination. "I don't have my best friend and husband anymore." She focused on the bag and punched repeatedly. "He left me to deal with everything and it's tough. Tougher than it should be."

"And I don't have a dad anymore." Cameron punched the bag harder using both hands, each strike a little harder than before. "I have no one to play ball with or go fishing with or talk to."

"That's it. Let it out." Along with Cameron and Holly, Ethan continued to strike the bag in a staccato rhythm. Moisture gathered on his forehead and under his arms with the action. Soon, the white walls began to collapse in on him, suffocating him in the memories of that day in Afghanistan and the recurrent dreams every night. "And each time I look at my hand

I know that I failed at my job. I let five people die because I wasn't paying attention."

"Why did you have to die on me? Why? I need you." Cameron yelled at the top of his lungs as he continually punched the bag and released some of the pent-up emotions he'd hidden away since his father's death. "Why did you have to die?"

Ethan caught Holly's stricken look as tears crested in her eyes before she fled the room. Somehow Ethan knew there had to be more than just survivor's guilt going on.

Chapter Five

Holly wiped her hands across her jeans and stared at her handiwork in the parlor Saturday afternoon. Somehow in just over seven hours, she'd transformed the mayor's three main living areas in his home into a Christmas wonderland. Of course, it helped having Ethan and Cam there to assist her with the last two. Her gaze wandered to where they stood by the tree, hanging the last of the blue and silver ornaments.

The changes she'd seen in her son in the week since he'd been going to Ethan's to help out every day after school were amazing. Her helpful, courteous and thoughtful son had returned, and Holly hadn't received one phone call from the principal. Cameron could continue to help out after school indefinitely, as long as that was what Ethan wanted.

Gathering her hair back into a ponytail again, she secured it with a hair tie as the scent of the newly cut tree filled her nose. Holly loved the crisp, outdoorsy aroma of pine trees. Sure, they were a mess and a fake one was more convenient, but other than the scent of gingerbread cookies baking in the oven, nothing conveyed the holiday season more.

A sense of accomplishment filled her as did a moment of melancholy.

The Christmas season had always had a special meaning for her. A renewal of sorts with the celebration of the birth of Jesus. Jared had felt the same way, which was one of the reasons he'd opened the store. Keeping the meaning of the season in their hearts had been important to him, and something she'd lost.

Her son, too.

The laughter had disappeared, lost on an icy road on a dark, wintry night. Pain tried to form inside her, but she pushed it away. She wouldn't allow the feeling to take over and ruin what promised to be a fun evening. Holly deserved it. Cam especially deserved it, and so did Ethan, since he would be joining them.

Somehow they'd all managed to survive, yet each of them carried around a guilt that clung to them like cling wrap. Sometimes the harder she worked at trying to straighten out her emotions, the more involved she became in them. Patience was the key, and she struggled with it on a daily basis. Especially lately. She closed her eyes, breathed deeply and sent up a silent prayer, something she'd been doing a lot more of this week, and it felt good. The first time had been hard, but it grew easier each time she tried. Comfort washed over her.

She glanced in Ethan's direction and saw an ornament slip out of his injured hand and hit the ground, breaking into two pieces. A look of disgust passed over his features as he stared at his hand. Holly knew he struggled with his own survivor's guilt and wondered why God had chosen this path for Ethan. One step forward in renewing her faith, two steps backward.

"No worries. We have plenty." Before Ethan could bend down, Holly walked over and scooped up the broken pieces and tucked them into her jeans pocket. Her heart went out to him again. Despite their workouts with the punching bag, neither one of them had been able to completely shed the pain from their pasts.

She smiled and picked up another ornament from the box. Energy coursed through her when their hands touched, and she pulled back. Ethan both confused and scared her. She wasn't looking for anyone else. Holly had already lost the love of her life. She couldn't handle another emotional involvement anytime soon.

"We could—"

"Always pull a few from the back of the tree if necessary." Ethan finished the sentence and Holly squirmed.

"That's what I thought, but they have so many, I think we should leave some of them in the box so we can actually see the tree."

Ethan's expression stilled as he descended from the first rung of the stepladder and moved in front of her. His gaze searched hers, as if trying to see past her layers of protection she'd wrapped around her heart. Conflicting emotions warred inside her, none of which she was willing to identify.

"I agree. Why bother with a real tree if you can't see it through the decorations?" He turned away from her and put the small, empty ornament containers back into their plastic storage boxes then glanced around the room. "Nice job, Holly. Once people see this, you're going to be getting a bunch of phone calls."

"Thanks." She attributed her breathlessness to all the work she'd done today and nothing more. It didn't matter that they'd worked well together, anticipating each other's needs, or that their conversations delved more into a familiarity that she'd only experienced once before with a man.

None of that mattered.

"You're welcome." His gaze focused on hers again, shutting out the music, the lights and everything else around them. Ethan opened and shut his mouth, clenched his fists and then turned away. "Come on, Cameron, time to put on the finishing touch."

Holly took her cue from Ethan. Concentrating on the here and now, and nothing else, she surveyed the rest of the room. Pride filled her. She had done a great job. Pine garlands covered with large white flowers and bows, clear lights, and blue and silver glass balls draped over the curtains and complimented the arrangement dominating the fireplace mantel.

White ceramic swans filled with more of the same white flowers and silver spray-painted twigs graced the tabletops. Tonight the white and silver candles would be lit, adding more charm and ambience to the room, along with the clear lights on the tree, where Ethan and Cameron were putting the finishing touches on the sixteen-foot-tall pine. Decorated with the same color scheme, it tied everything together.

She had transformed the room into a Christmas wonderland.

Holly's heart skipped a beat, though, as Cameron clambered up the ladder with the tree topper. "Cam—"

She bit down on her lip to keep the rest of her words inside when her son turned around and stared at her. He'd been a real trouper with all the decorating and had even come up with a few ideas himself of where things should be placed. He'd inherited both her and Jared's artistic talents. Cam wasn't a little boy anymore, and she had to remember that there was a teenager inside struggling to get out. She had to let him find his way even though she wanted to remind him to be careful. "You're doing great. Thanks for all your help today."

"We're still going to the festival today, right?"

Typical response. Cam was only helping her so they could go to the festival, but it still gladdened her heart that he wanted to spend time with her. Although she detected a bit of hero worship when he looked at Ethan. "Of course. I can't wait."

"Hang on a second, Cameron. Let me hold the ladder for you. I'm sure a trip to the E.R. is not what your mom has in mind for tonight if you fall." As if sensing her distress, Ethan walked over and held on to Cameron's legs to steady him as her son placed the ornate silver star at the top.

The fact that they had similar thoughts scared

Holly. Because if she ever contemplated dating again or getting involved with another man, some of Ethan Pellegrino's characteristics would top the list of things she would look for.

"Done. Let's go." Oblivious to the emotions of the people around him, Cam scrambled down the ladder.

"Oh, Holly, it looks stunning." Edith Moss joined her. "I especially like the silver twigs. I would have never thought that bringing more of the outdoors inside would create such a charming setting. I'll make sure everyone knows that you did my decorating this year. I'm sure you'll get several clients, especially since this is so early in the season. But you know how crazy things get after Thanksgiving. This was the only time that worked for us."

"Thanks, Mrs. Moss. I appreciate the opportunity."

"No. Thank you. I can't tell you how relieved I am that it's finished. Now I can concentrate on the other things."

"Like the food." Mayor Moss rubbed his round belly as he joined his wife. Around them, caterers and staff busied themselves with the food setup.

Holly smiled at the portly mayor, whose adoring attention was on his wife. Married thirty-some years, and he still looked at her the same way he probably had the day they exchanged their vows. Something Holly wouldn't experience, because she and Jared had only made the ten-year mark. Yet she didn't begrudge them their happiness, and maybe someday, she'd experience love again, if she could let go of the past. If she wanted to go there.

Looking away, Holly clutched the envelope Mayor Moss had given her and tucked it into her purse. "All right, boys, let's put all the boxes back into storage and go. The Fall Harvest Festival is waiting."

The community center building teemed with life as they entered through the double doors twenty minutes later. Music from one of the local bands filled the air with the beat of a current hit, as did the scent of freshly popped popcorn.

Games lined the far side of the room and bounce houses for the smaller kids dominated the gymnasium to their right. Food vendors had set up along the back wall with the band and dance area stationed to their left.

"I see a friend of mine. Can I have some money?" Cam looked at her, hope, expectation and a tiny bit of trepidation in his eyes.

"Which one?"

"Tyler." Cam's gaze darted past her shoulder.

Holly's mouth went dry at the thought of the sixty dollars in her wallet because she hadn't gotten to the bank to deposit her check from the mayor. Forty of those dollars had been ear-marked for groceries and the rest for the festival. Somehow she thought they'd spend it together, but her son seemed to have other ideas despite what he'd told her at Ethan's house Monday. Holly had known the day was coming when Cam would rather spend the time with his friends instead of her, but it still hurt.

"Okay." She opened her wallet and pulled out a ten-dollar bill. Cam had helped out quite a bit this afternoon, and Holly hadn't given him his allowance yet for the few chores he'd done this week. He deserved to have some fun with his friend. "Check back in an hour."

"How about two?" Cam slipped past her.

When Holly turned around, though, she saw her son walking toward a group of boys from school that didn't include his friend Tyler Adamson. Her shoulders sagged when she recognized the ringleader of the group. She should have guessed that Cam had an ulterior motive for coming here today. The low-slung pants on the four other boys, the ripped T-shirts and the baseball caps positioned to the side made her stomach churn. The furtive glances in her direction didn't help her nerves, either.

Ethan's gaze followed hers, and he placed his hand on her arm, creating that familiar tingling sensation in her stomach. "Do you want me to stop him?"

"No. I don't think causing a scene would be a good thing right now."

"Agreed. Let's see what kind of choices he decides to make tonight. One of them is Patrick, isn't it?"

"The one in charge. Two boys I can't identify, but underneath the long, uncombed hair, I recognize Tyler Smith, one of Cam's friends from grade school. I guess I should have asked which Tyler he was referring to. I don't understand how Cam fell in with that crowd."

"Sometimes it depends on where they are in their life at any particular moment." Ethan spoke as if he had personal experience, and Holly knew it to be true from their conversation while painting his garage door.

She waited for Ethan to elaborate and sighed as she watched Cam and his friends nod and knuckle-bang each other before they disappeared into the crowd. Holly wanted to follow, yet something in Ethan's gaze held her back. Cameron had already made a poor choice with Patrick and had paid the consequence. She could only hope that he'd learned from his mistake.

"So, I guess that leaves the two of us." Ethan

gave her a half smile as his gaze lingered on the spot where Cam had just stood. Concern and hesitation clouded his expression.

"It does. For now. I don't trust those boys." Holly could feel they were on the same wavelength. The thought gladdened her and scared her. It felt good to share her concerns with Ethan, but opening up an area in her heart again could only lead to more pain. And yet with Cameron getting older and wanting to spend less time with her, the idea that she didn't want to spend the rest of her life alone erupted in her mind. The earlier image of Mayor and Mrs. Moss and how happy they were didn't help, either. Tonight she was going to forget about everything else and have fun.

"Me, neither. What would you like to do?"

"Let's walk around and take a look at all the activities first. Since Mrs. Sanderson took over, there's bound to be a few surprises." Holly moved into the stream of traffic, needing to surround herself with other people besides Ethan and the strange emotions he had awakened inside her.

Coming to the festival had been a good idea in theory, but it had been her and Cam when she'd imagined it, not her son running off with a group of so-called friends and leaving her with Ethan. From the looks and the number of people who stopped to talk to them, though, the town gossips were going to have a lot to talk about tomorrow. She threw caution to the wind. It had been a long time since she'd really had fun, and she was glad Ethan was here with her.

"Looks like the bouncy castles are a big hit." Piles of shoes thrown haphazardly outside the Princess Castle and Dinosaur House along with the squeals of young children confirmed that.

"Cameron used to love those." They walked by a crowded craft table containing the materials to make sand art in a plastic bottle. Holly recognized a few of the younger kids from church and smiled at their parents. "He also loved making things. I still have one of his sand creations in my china cabinet. Now all he seems to make is trouble. Well, up until last week, that is. His turnaround is remarkable. Thank you."

"You're welcome. He's a pleasure to be around. I think he's going to be just fine."

"I hope so." Holly wasn't sure how much more stress she could handle, even though things seemed to have gotten better in the past week, thanks to Ethan's intervention. And maybe, just maybe, God was listening to her prayers and they were starting to work.

"He will." He grabbed her hand and squeezed it gently. "Let's try the cake walk." Ethan pulled her to the booth that contained a table laden with various cakes and pies. "We can still get in on this round."

He handed two tickets from the ten he'd bought earlier to the woman standing next to the boom box and motioned for Holly to step on a numbered circle behind his. The music started and both Holly and Ethan moved from one circle to the next. Holly laughed as she jumped into his circle. He turned, his hands grazing her waist to keep her from falling over. "No fair. This is my circle."

His touch exhilarated and frightened her and she hadn't felt this carefree in a long time. Playfully, she pushed him from the circle. "Keep moving. You can't hog it all to yourself."

"If that's the way you want to play."

But before Ethan could make his move, Holly jumped away and ahead of him to the next circle, the music keeping time with the tempo of her heart. More laughter filled the air as she moved from circle to circle, only once glancing back to catch a smiling Ethan looking at her. She turned away but not until after she returned his grin.

Just a few more hops and she'd be back to her favorite number. The music stopped just as she reached nine. The woman running the booth pulled out a number from her paper bag. "Number nine is the winner."

"Holly, that's you." Ethan stepped over and high-fived her.

"Yes. Cam will be so excited." Holly put her name on the chocolate-mousse cake to collect before they left, an extravagant dessert she would never allow herself to buy because of the cost. "And because you bought the ticket, we can all share this tonight after the festival closes."

"Sounds like a plan. So how do you feel about bobbing for apples?" Ethan pointed to the next booth over, where adults behaved like kids as they dunked their heads into the big horse trough filled with water.

"Go for it."

"Only if you do it with me. It looks like they're giving away some pretty good prizes." He pointed to the sign behind the trough. "I wonder if anyone's won the $100 gift card yet."

Holly didn't want to get her face wet and chance her mascara giving her raccoon eyes, but the idea that she could win a generic gift card that could be used at any number of stores caught her eye. She could use it to help buy the present that Cameron longed for this year.

"You're on." She looked around the crowded room again in an attempt to locate her son but only managed to catch the attention of her neighbors. She smiled and waved but this time managed to hand the booth attendant two of the tickets she'd bought before Ethan could.

"Okay, no use of hands or feet or any other body part is allowed," the volunteered droned. "No getting help from your neighbor, either."

Ethan winked at her. "There goes that idea."

Holly blushed under his scrutiny. "Why, Ethan, you didn't strike me as someone who broke the rules."

"Let's just say I like to think outside the box. Which one do you think I should try for?"

"How about the green one in front of you. It doesn't look too battered."

"The green one it is, then."

A few moments later, Holly wiped the water from her face after having come up empty in her attempt. The apples were hard to get a grip on, and the harder she tried, the more the apples seemed to mock her attempt. Ethan, on the other hand, was still trying to snag the green one. She watched in fascination as he managed to grab the stem of the apple and pull it from the water. Holly wasn't exactly sure if that was the correct way to play, but she clapped and cheered along with the rest of the crowd.

"Let's see what you won." She took the apple from him and compared the colored thumbtack pushed in the bottom to the chart on the sign. "Well, it's not the $100 card, but it looks like you're the proud owner of a $15 certificate to Marc's Hobby World."

"Terrific. You can use it as a stocking stuffer for Cameron."

Holly handed Ethan the towel she'd just used to wipe her face. His words made her breath catch in her throat. The selfless action sent a jolt into her bloodstream that refused to still, but she needed to refuse. He was already doing enough for her by letting her stay in the shop and assisting with Cameron, whom she hadn't seen since the evening began.

"Better yet, why don't *you* give it to Cameron for all the help he's doing for you. Here, you missed a spot." Using the corner of the towel, she reached up and dabbed the droplet of water clinging to his sideburn. The action, so innocent on her part, seemed to change something between them as they stared at each other, the noise and the people fading into the background. "Finish drying off. I'll go collect your prize."

Ethan stared after Holly as she slipped away.

"Ethan Pellegrino. I'd heard you were back. Good to see you again."

Glad for the distraction, Ethan turned toward the voice and recognized his former classmate immediately. Whatever had just happened between him and Holly needed to be stopped. He had other things to think about, like his dog shelter, learning to work with his right hand again, learning to trust his instincts so he didn't make another fatal mistake. "Jeremy Foster. How's it going?"

"Not too bad. Yourself?"

Ethan took in Jeremy's police uniform. Somehow his old high-school friend's career choice surprised him. Jeremy had had a bit of a wild streak in him as well, and they'd both had their share of scrapes with adults in the past. But then again, who better to understand the youth in this town?

"Glad to be home for good. What's with the uniform? I thought you were more interested in politics."

"Still am, but from a different perspective now. Who knows, though. Maybe I'll run for police chief once Phillips retires."

"He's still around?" The police chief had been old before Ethan left for the service. The man should be well past retirement age and planted on one of the community benches lining Main Street along with all the other retirees.

"Yeah, he plans on dropping dead in his office with his uniform on."

"That doesn't surprise me."

Holly returned and handed him his gift certificate, but before she could slip away again,

Ethan put his hand on her arm. "Have you met Holly Stanwyck?"

"Can't say that I have. Pleased to meet you. Jeremy Foster."

"You, too." Holly shook his hand and smiled tentatively.

Ethan didn't appreciate the length of time it took Jeremy to release Holly's hand even though Ethan had no claim to her heart. "Anything interesting going on in town?"

With one more casual glance at Holly, Jeremy focused back on Ethan, his professionalism returning. "Just the usual, although there seems to be a lot more vandalism and mischief happening. Word has it it's a bunch of kids. If you see or hear anything, let me know."

"Will do." Ethan glanced over and saw that the blood had drained from Holly's face. She'd obviously connected the incident with his garage door. Could the issues be related?

"I'd better run. I'm on the clock. Again, it was nice to meet you, Holly. Call me if Pellegrino gets out of line." With that, Jeremy strode away into the waning crowd.

"I wonder where Cam wandered off to." Holly broke the silence between them.

Ethan's gaze searched the room. Cameron and the other boys were nowhere to be seen. During the hour they'd been there, he'd kept his eye out for Holly's son. He hadn't seen him in a while, and his gut told him they were not in the building. "Let's go check outside."

"Outside?"

"I doubt they're inside one of the bouncy castles."

After stepping into the cool, crisp night, Ethan took her arm and guided her along the sidewalk that led to the parking lot. But instead of heading toward the lighted area where all the cars were parked, he strode in the other direction, away from the lights and people.

The smell of cigarette smoke assaulted his nostrils once they reached the back of the building. In the darkness, an orange glow hovered in the air, as if passed around from hand to hand. In the shadows, he made out a group of six figures, one of them most likely Holly's son.

Holly gasped. "Cameron wouldn't, would he?"

"We're about to find out. Cameron Stanwyck, show yourself."

"Run." A boy's hushed tone broke the stillness. Shadows melted into the night and footsteps pounded against the blacktop.

Ethan managed to filter out which was Holly's son and step in front of him to keep him from running.

"Cam, what were you doing out here?"

Holly's strangled voice thrust a knife through Ethan's heart. Her vulnerability when it came to her son affected him on a more personal level than he cared to admit. He wasn't the boy's father, but Ethan felt a responsibility to Holly, Jared and the community to keep Cameron from making the same mistakes he had.

"I wasn't doing anything."

"No? Then what's this?" Ethan kicked at a cigarette butt.

"The other boys were doing it. I was just standing here."

Ethan sniffed. At least it was only cigarette smoke he smelled, but given what he'd seen of the other boys, something stronger was probably going to follow sooner rather than later. It didn't matter the size of the town—drugs and alcohol abuse were everywhere. He stepped closer. Ethan's intervention with Cameron had come just in time. "Try again."

"Ethan, stop. Please." Holly placed her hand on his arm. "This is my problem."

He knew he was treading on Holly's parenting skills, but even in the dim light, he could see that all the blood had leeched from her face again. Moisture pooled in her eyes and the skin between her brows furrowed.

"Not anymore."

"Yes, it is." She fisted her hands and planted

them on her waist. "Cameron, we will discuss this on the way home. Now, go to the car."

"Look, Holly, it's not just cigarettes. They've been drinking." He pointed to the ground by Cameron's feet. "Before you get in the car, pick up the empty bottles and go throw them in the trash."

Cameron didn't say a word confirming or denying the truth as he collected the bottles and slunk toward the trash can nearby.

"Are you undermining my authority, Ethan? I'm Cameron's parent, not you." Anger simmered beneath her breath.

"I'm well aware of that, but there's nothing wrong with getting some help. What do you think would have happened if Officer Foster had found the boys? Especially since alcohol was involved."

"I believe my son when he tells me that he was just standing there."

Ethan scraped his hand through his hair. "Do you know anything about guilt by association?"

Holly sighed. "No." Her shoulders slumped again. "I feel like such a failure."

"You are not a failure, Holly. Far from it." He tucked a loose strand of hair behind Holly's ear, the gesture sending a wave of compassion and the need to protect her through him. He leaned in a fraction, his gaze lingering on her lips. What was he thinking? Neither he nor Holly needed that complication right now. He valued their tentative friendship that he hoped could survive the eviction after next month. "You've done a great job with him. But he's at that tough age where he's testing his limits and your patience. You have enough to worry about. Please let me help."

Holly stared at him and finally nodded as a silent Cameron returned and kicked at a small rock on the blacktop.

Ethan crossed his arms and faced him. "You have a decision to make, son. Your fair-weather friends, who have obviously already turned on you since they're no longer here, or the dogs. Think long and hard about what each of them means to you and let me know. You can't have both."

Chapter Six

Soft light filtered through the front window of the shop as Holly sat behind the counter mid-afternoon Monday. Outside, city workers strung holiday lights on the trees across the street in the town square and on the trees lining the sidewalks. Colorful red and green banners hung from the streetlights, adding an even more festive feel along with the large Christmas tree filled with ornaments of different shapes and colors. Each of the businesses, Holly's included, had hung exterior Christmas lights around their windows, adding to the quaint feel of the small town.

Too bad the mood outside didn't reflect the one inside her shop, despite the dwindling merchandise. Yesterday's sales had emptied more shelf space, but it wasn't enough. She was too far in debt to remain open and keep Jared's dream alive. The bare Christmas tree in the corner sported a new for-sale sign, and in between customers she'd spent the past hour rearranging all the figurines, wooden nutcrackers and candleholders into more visible positions.

Despite the lights, the music and the scent of the holidays, the Christmas spirit had passed over her this year.

Holly pulled up Cameron's grades online, rubbed her eyes and stared at the computer screen. She had more immediate things to worry about. How had Cam's grades dropped even further? When she'd checked just over a week ago, they'd been Bs and Cs. Now they were Cs and Ds. Cameron had always been a good student.

She'd failed her son. In fact, she didn't even know him anymore. How had he gotten involved with Patrick and his cigarette-smoking, beer-drinking buddies? Despite her talk with Cam after church yesterday, Holly didn't know if he'd been serious when he'd chosen the dogs over his so-called friends.

Another Christmas carol drifted around her in the stillness of the shop, and even the scent of pine brought her no comfort today. For the first time since they'd opened the shop, Holly turned around and slammed the radio off. She couldn't handle it any more than she could stand to see the twinkling lights making the remaining leaves shimmer across the street. With Thanksgiving only a week away and more and more phone calls about her decorating business coming in, her days and nights were stretched thin, and tonight she was supposed to go see the winner of the church auction. She now had less time for her son, especially since she didn't see him right after school anymore. Was that why his grades suffered?

Clicking into each individual teacher's highlighted name, she stared at the number of missing or incomplete assignments. More caged butterflies begged to be released from her stomach. "But he's done them. I know he has. Why hasn't he turned them in?"

Holly dropped her head into the palms of her hands. *Where did I go wrong, Lord?*

Sometimes she felt so alone.

It wasn't supposed to be this way. Her clenched hands banged down on the spot on the counter where the stain had worn away over the years and rattled the pens. God was supposed to be there for her. So where was He? She'd been reaching out again, but even He abandoned her. Why did she even bother? She knew the answer. Cameron. And maybe, just maybe, despite it all, a small piece of her still believed.

If God wouldn't talk to her, she knew someone who would. Holly picked up the phone and dialed Kristen. While she waited for her friend to answer, Holly cradled the receiver and picked up the pen holder her son had made for her in first grade. She ran her fingers along the ripples of the old soup can where he'd glued a hand-drawn stick figure of Santa along with colorful wrapping paper to cover the tin. Another speck of paint chipped off the bottom, reminding her that nothing lasted forever. Nothing. With stiff fingers, she brushed it to the floor and set the pen holder back by the register.

"What's up, girlfriend?" a breathless Kristen answered. In the background, Holly heard her friend's three-year-old banging on what sounded like a pot. She winced at the noise, remembering those days well. Her friend sounded flustered.

"Nothing. Sounds like you're busy."

"I'm never too busy for you. Wait a second till I plant the kids in front of the TV for a few minutes. I'll be right back."

"Okay." Holly twisted the phone cord until the room grew silent, her gaze wandering outside the large storefront window, and caught sight of a dead leaf clinging to a branch, yet fluttering helplessly in the breeze. Holly knew how the leaf felt, if it had that ability. *Hold on, little fella. You can do it.* But seconds later, a gust tore the leaf from its mooring and carried it away.

Holly refused to suffer the same fate. Unlike the leaf, her destiny wasn't so short-lived, and despite closing the shop at the end of the year, she'd make things work out. She'd also figure out how to deal with her son and get his grades back up.

"I'm back. So what's wrong?" Kristen asked.

Holly's confidence faded, though, as she stared at the computer screen again and pushed the print icon.

"Cam's about ready to fail this semester."

"Uh-oh. What do you mean?"

"I just checked his grades. They've gone down since last week. He's not turning in his homework. There's only four weeks left, and I don't know if he can bring them back up to A's and B's or if he even wants to. His attitude really stinks right now."

"But I thought that Ethan was making sure his homework was done before Cam worked with the dogs."

"He is, and I check Cam's agenda and work almost every night." Holly twirled a section of hair around her finger. At this rate, she'd have a bald spot by Christmas. "I've been so worried about the store and keeping a roof over Cam's head that I've failed him. I don't know my son anymore, and that hurts worst of all."

"You haven't failed him, Holly. This is just one of those stages. He's about to hit his teen years. Something else is going on. Go talk to Ethan. You need to get this taken care of right away. Just give me a few minutes to pack the kids in the car and I'll be right over to watch the shop."

"I can't let you do that."

"Yes, you can. Tony's at work and dinner's in the Crock-Pot. The kids love 'Tis Always the Season. It'll give them a change of scenery. I'm not taking no for an answer."

Twenty minutes later, Holly pulled up slowly to Ethan's house and saw both the man and the dog Bear walking up the middle of the driveway. Catching him unawares gave her a few moments to study him. Ethan was taller than Jared but had the same slim build. His hair was a bit darker, and now that it was growing out from the military cut, she noticed the curls. But that wasn't what made her pull her bottom lip between her teeth.

His slumped shoulders and slow gait as he glanced through the mail that he'd retrieved from his mailbox spoke of a man with his own set of problems and worries. She knew the feeling well and found herself wanting to put her hand in his and squeeze gently to let him know he wasn't alone, but that would place her in an emotional position she didn't want to be in. She had enough to deal with already, and putting herself back out there would only lead to more pain.

She pulled up next to him, rolled down her window and then breathed in the cool, crisp air, laden with another hint of winter. "Hi, Ethan."

"Holly?" A surprised Ethan glanced up from the stack of mail. "What are you doing here?" Creases formed between his eyes, and his lips curved downward, accentuating his five-o'clock shadow as he leaned through the window. "Cameron's not coming?"

"He said he was, but I'm not sure anymore." Holly swallowed and managed to keep the emotion from her voice. Breaking down in front of Ethan was not an option. Not when she knew he'd put her first. They were friendly to each other because of Cameron and the store, nothing more, despite the fact her heartbeat accelerated a bit, like it was doing right now. With all her other distractions, she hadn't really noticed how handsome he was. Well, maybe she had just a little.

Her gaze drifted to his right hand. Even that didn't bother her quite as much as before, yet as he stared down where she'd looked moments earlier, she knew he hadn't forgotten her reaction to his injury.

"What's going on?" The frown still tugged at his lips.

"I'd like to show you something. Hang on." She placed the car in Park, unbuckled the seat belt and turned off the ignition. After Ethan moved away from the door, she grabbed her purse and stepped out, glad her friend had convinced her to see him. Kristen was right. Since Ethan monitored Cam's homework before her son could work with the dogs, he had a vested interest in his grades. If they didn't improve, Holly would stop the arrangement.

He held up his mail. "Let's go inside. My hands are a bit full." Once Ethan dumped the stack on the kitchen table, he turned to Holly. "What did you want to show me?"

"Cam's grades. I pulled them off the grade portal." She gave him the paper and set her fists on her hips. Inhaling sharply, she caught the scent of freshly baked chocolate-chip cookies and dog. "I don't understand what's going on."

Ethan's brow furrowed even more as he rubbed the back of his neck. His eyes widened and his lips pursed. "I don't, either." His gaze captured hers, pulling more oxygen from her lungs. The sincere tone of his voice told her more than his words. "He has done his homework."

"I know he has. I check almost nightly." Holly sank into the kitchen chair and rested her forehead against her palm. The confusion in her stomach went north and created havoc in her brain. Something had changed between them Saturday, and despite what her brain wanted, her feelings and emotions wanted something else. Or to at least explore the possibilities. Her blood chilled as she stared up at the man who'd suddenly made her want things again.

"Something else must be going on."

"But what?"

Ethan glanced at his watch as he strode around the cramped room. "If Cameron is coming here, we'll know in about five minutes. If he doesn't show up, then it may take a bit longer, because we'll have to go find him."

Holly appreciated his words. Maybe that was why she'd come here in the first place. She could have dealt with the situation with her son at home and over the phone with Ethan. And yet, she'd wanted to see him, talk to him, just be near him.

"Would you like a chocolate-chip cookie? Fresh out of the oven." Ethan changed the subject and held out a blue plastic plate.

Her stomach growled at the tantalizing smell,

reminding her she hadn't eaten anything since breakfast, her lunch still in the mini refrigerator at the store. "You baked them?"

"I'm crushed that you think I'm helpless in the kitchen. I can bake. Sort of." He gave her a slight grin. "Okay, so I used a package from the refrigerated section, but it's the thought that counts, right?"

"Of course. I'd love one. All I need now is a glass of milk." Add her grandmother's lilac scent and she'd be transported back to the simpler days of her childhood.

"That can be arranged." Ethan set the plate down in front of her and pulled three glasses from the cabinet. Then he retrieved the milk and poured some into two of the glasses. "I'll pour Cameron's when he gets here."

Holly bit into the warm cookie and let the chocolate burst across her tongue. How long had it been since she'd had the time to do something as simple as baking cookies? Too long. Since before Jared's death. She hadn't even cheated by using a frozen or refrigerated package from the store like Ethan did. These days she relied on packaged cookies from the store shelves for Cam's lunches.

She stared as Ethan dunked his in the milk first and then took a bite. "What? This is the only way to eat them."

"You know, I like milk and chocolate-chip cookies, just not together like that. I don't even like root-beer floats, but I do like root beer and vanilla ice cream separately."

"You don't know what you're missing." He popped the rest of it into his mouth. "Sometimes we even put in cream soda or, my personal favorite, orange soda. It tasted just like those things we used to buy from the ice-cream man who drove around the neighborhood every weekend."

"The ice-cream man. Wow. I haven't thought of him for years. They used to have someone who drove around during the summer, but I haven't seen him lately." Holly savored another bite. "These are pretty good for not making your own dough. I remember making chocolate-chip cookies from scratch with my grandmother. She was a traditionalist. We even sifted the flour before we put it in."

"Yeah, my grandmother was like that, too. There's something to be said about the time before cell phones, three hundred television channels and handheld computer games."

The sound of footsteps clomping up the back steps caught her attention right before the back door opened and Cameron careened inside. "Mom? What are you doing here? Who's watching the store?"

Ethan took a step back and busied himself with pouring a glass of milk.

"Kristen is at the shop right now. There's something I need to discuss with you, and it couldn't wait until after dinner. I pulled a copy of your current grades off-line this afternoon. Is there something we need to talk about?"

Cam refused to make eye contact and kicked the floor with the toe of his shoe. "No."

"Then how do you explain your grades?"

"Can I go see the dogs, Mr. P.?"

"No." Ethan glanced at Holly as he set the milk and the cookies on the table. If he had to choose an adjective or two, he'd describe her as *vulnerable* and *lost*. Not a good combination, because it brought out that need to protect her again. "You need to answer your mother. I won't tolerate any disrespect, remember?"

Cameron glanced at him before he exploded on his mother. "Fine. I hate school. I hate homework. And sometimes I even hate you. I wish you had died instead of Dad."

"What?" Holly gasped and sank back in her seat. All color fled her cheeks, and shock pulled her jaw open. Tears gathered in her eyes, causing Ethan's instincts to overload. He had to get a handle on this situation before it spiraled further out of control.

"Sit down." Ethan yanked out a chair. The

boy needed some heavier intervention and fast. He seethed. Where had Cameron learned this type of behavior? No one should ever be on the receiving end of those words. "You will never speak to your mother like that. Do you understand me?"

Out of the corner of his eye he saw Holly clench her fingers and stand. "I can handle this, Ethan. Cameron, put your backpack on. We're going home."

"But I don't wanna go home." Cameron flew into his mother's arms. "I'm sorry, Mom. I didn't mean it. I love you. It's just so hard—"

Holly cradled him back. "I know, sweetie. I know. I'm sorry that I haven't been there for you like I should have been. Like I should be. Why don't you come back to the shop and do your homework there, like the old days? Just me and you and some hot chocolate."

"Because I like it here. I like the dogs. I like Mr. P. I want to come here after school."

"Then what's going on with your grades, Cam? They're all C's and D's."

The boy remained silent.

"When I opened up each subject, most of your homework was missing. You did it all. I know because I checked it. What did you do with it?"

The only sound in the room was their breathing and the whining of the kenneled dogs.

"I think I know what's happening." Ethan paced the small area. Someone was bullying Cameron. The accusation would be a strong one, but he wasn't about to let Holly and Jared's son flunk seventh grade. "Patrick's been taking your work and turning it in as his own, hasn't he?"

The boy held his mother tighter. Ethan captured Holly's tortured gaze, her pale skin and large eyes. Knots twisted his gut as he wrestled with what decision to make. He'd been wrong before, couldn't trust his own judgment half the time, yet somehow he knew he wasn't wrong about this.

"I bet he also told you that if you told anyone, he'd beat you up. What's Patrick's last name?" A sinking feeling developed in the pit of his stomach. There'd been a similar incident between some boys when he'd been in middle school.

"Dennison."

"And I bet his dad's name is William." His feelings were justified. "Did it happen again today?"

Cameron shook his head. "There was no homework last weekend. I tried to stay away from him today after what happened Saturday night, but he followed me around. He wouldn't leave me alone and kept calling me names."

"I'll go talk to your principal tomorrow, Cam. I won't allow this to continue." Holly kissed the top of his head.

A look of relief flitted across her son's face. "Will you go, too, Mr. P.? Principal Buchanan is mean and old. He might scare my mom."

"Cameron. Mr. Buchanan and I get along fine."

"Please? I want him to go, Mom. He is the one helping me with my homework."

"Is that what you want?" Pain laced her voice and deepened the green of her eyes.

When Cameron nodded, Ethan caught the adulation on Cameron's face as he glanced at him. By her sharp intake of air, he realized Holly caught it, too. When Ethan had come up with the idea of Cameron helping out with the dogs, he'd never intended for the boy to bond with him. Holly's son needed to find a different father figure, one who could keep him safe. "This is something your mom needs to take care of, Cameron."

"Please?"

Great. Being manipulated by a twelve-year-old was a bit unnerving. "Only if she wants me to."

"Please, Mom?"

"If that's what you want and if Mr. Pellegrino is free, then he can come with me."

Ethan was glad to see that he wasn't the only one feeling cornered. "Let's see what you've got for homework today. After you're done, I've decided that instead of working around here, I'll take you out to the real sanctuary and show you around. Holly, you're welcome to join us unless you need to go back to the shop."

"I'd like that. Let me ask Kristen if she can close up."

"But what about everything we have to do?"

"You do your homework, Cam, and I'll do your chores so we can leave as soon as possible. I think after a day like today, we all need to have a little break." Holly glanced over Cameron's head at him, her expression closed just a fraction.

In that moment, he realized that Holly had interpreted her son's wants correctly and she wanted to keep them from spending too much time together alone. It was as if they were a family, not too different from the one he'd established with his patrol back in the Middle East. The kitchen shrank under the weight of the responsibility he wasn't sure he wanted. Because then he had to protect them. But could he when he didn't even trust that he could protect himself?

* * *

"This is it. The final home for Beyond the Borders Dog Sanctuary." Ethan turned off the county highway and into the long, winding driveway defined by tall ash, sycamore and pine trees. Swatches of fall color still clung to the remaining leaves, and a hint of smoke from a neighbor's fireplace drifted through the air. Last week's snow had melted but had left muddy patches in the ruts where the gravel had disappeared over the years.

"Wow. It's beautiful," Holly marveled. "It's hard to believe we're only fifteen minutes from town."

"Do you get a lot of deer out here?"

"Deer, elk and an occasional cougar or bear." At Holly's soft gasp, Ethan leaned over and patted her hand. Mistake. He found himself wanting to hold it, which would be impossible. Her hand moved under his, bringing back the memory of her revulsion of his injuries. He pulled away. "Don't worry. It's been a while since we've seen any other wildlife besides rabbits and coyotes."

At the last bend in the driveway, the old two-story farmhouse came into view. A fresh coat of white paint covered the wood siding, and the dark red shutters on either side of the four windows complemented the front door. Two benches and a rocking chair graced the porch running the entire front of the house, and an empty birdbath added a homier feel to the home Ethan's great-grandfather had built.

Brown dotted patches of the front lawn, but next spring and summer, he envisioned replacing the shrubbery in the front and adding some flowers, as well. He'd have to ask Holly for her opinion. Repainting had been the easy part; he'd just followed what had already been done.

"It's gorgeous."

"Are you going to live out here, Mr. P.?" Cameron piped up from the backseat.

"Eventually." Ethan looked at Holly's son in the rearview mirror. "I'll want to be near the dogs once we make the move."

"What about your house in town?"

"I'll rent that out and use the money to pay the mortgage and my bills."

"That makes sense." Holly crossed her arms.

Ethan eased his car to a stop, his hands gripping the steering wheel a bit tighter than normal. The sensation felt odd because of his missing fingers, but that would just be something else he had to get used to. The temperature inside the car had dropped noticeably with his insensitive words. If Holly wasn't paying the rent on the store, she probably had trouble making her mortgage payments, as well. He hoped that wasn't the case, because the thought of Holly and Cameron without a home didn't sit well, especially when he was lucky to have two. Well, the bank still owned part of one, and technically his mother owned this one, but by Holly's pale face and tight expression, the damage had already been done.

"This place is cool." Unknowingly, Cameron changed the subject when he jumped out of the car and ran toward the dormant grass between the house and the barn.

"Cam, wait." Holly struggled with the broken lock.

"Doesn't work." Ethan opened the door and helped her from the car. "Cameron will be fine. There's nothing out here that can hurt him." Setting his hand against the small of her back, he escorted her over the uneven ground where her son had run moments earlier. The action spoke of the possibility that there could be something between them if either one was looking for that. He knew Holly wasn't. He wasn't, either, but dropping his arm to his side left him feeling incomplete in a way that had nothing to do with his missing fingers.

He shook his head to clear his mind and focus on what should be the most important thing right now. "I'll show you the barn and runs first and then the inside of the house. Cameron, over here."

The traditional-looking two-story wood barn had also been treated to a new coat of red paint that matched the house. As Ethan pulled the barn door open, it creaked. A musky scent of old hay filled his nose, and darkness interrupted his vision until he flipped the switch to his right. A lone lightbulb suspended from the ceiling chased away most of the shadows. "This place needs to be rewired and a lot more lights added."

"Lights would be good. So would a bit of heat. I think it's colder in here than outside." Holly pulled her jacket closer.

"It probably is. Last night was pretty cold. Until I can afford to put in a central-heating and air-conditioning unit, I'll be using portable heaters and lots of old blankets in the kennels." Ethan walked to the center of the barn and surveyed the large, open space.

"Manny and his son have already demolished the horse stalls so I'll have room for twenty-four kennels, twelve along each side. The back will be for storage and up front, when I install some plumbing, will be the bathing area."

"Manny?"

"My handyman. His wife is sick so he took the day off to take her to the doctor."

"What are you going to use the upstairs for?" Cameron ran over to the rickety ladder leading to the loft.

"Be careful, Cam."

"Don't climb on that. It's not safe," Ethan ordered as the boy put his foot on the first rung. "I haven't decided yet. They used to store the hay up there, but maybe the cats will go up there."

"Cats?"

"My cousin has accepted a ferret, so cats aren't too far behind."

"Do you have a problem with cats?" Not appreciating his tone of voice, Holly crossed her arms and glared up at him.

Ethan scraped his hand through his hair, remembering that Holly had a cat. A cat Jared had brought home for her. He was scoring points left and right with her today. "Not at all, even though I can't say I understand them. They're just not my favorite of all God's creatures, and I'm not sure where to put them."

Holly relaxed. "Cats certainly keep you on your toes, that's for sure. Maybe you can convert one of the upstairs rooms of the house into a cattery. I don't think kenneling them here would work very well."

Holly's idea rattled around inside his brain. The old farmhouse had four bedrooms upstairs, and he only needed one. He could use one for the cats, another for any other type of creature—like the ferret or a reptile or bird—that showed up and still have one for a workout room. Plus he had the attic.

"That would probably work. Being as curious and agile as cats are, I'd have to enclose the loft, and if one of them got out, it could get interesting with all the dogs. Separate accommodations would be a good idea." And that was where Holly's expertise would come in, if she and Cameron stayed around. He had no idea how long the arrangement would last, but he hoped it would be awhile. The thought of not seeing her and her son almost every day left an empty hole in his heart. "Come on, let me show you what I've got planned for the outside."

He ushered them outside and took in what remained of autumn outlining the large backyard where the run would go. What little remained of fall contrasted with the pine trees interspersed among the deciduous ones and amazed him. He'd missed the change of seasons overseas, but God had really outdone himself this year. And continued to do so. From the snowfall they'd already experienced, it looked to be a winter with a lot of accumulation, especially in the higher elevations as he took in the white-capped mountains to his left.

Turning away from the beauty, he locked the

freshly painted barn door and realized he was going to need a security system on the house and the barn, too. More money he didn't have, but he had a lead on another grant.

Had he made a mistake in trying to take on such a big endeavor? There was still so much to do and more calls coming in about his sanctuary every week. Three more dogs were scheduled to arrive mid-January. He had to be ready. The alternative for the dogs wasn't an option.

Let go, let God.

No. He hadn't made a mistake. He felt it in his bones. All those hours in the hospital bed had given him plenty of time to think and reflect on his life and pray about what to do next. God had opened a new door for him. *New doors,* he thought as he watched Cameron run through the grassy area destined to become the play area for the dogs.

Mentoring boys on the edge of becoming delinquents had to be another part of that plan and would give him the extra volunteers that he needed to run a successful sanctuary.

"It's really beautiful out here. I'm sure the dogs will love it. This will be the dog run?"

"Yes. Manny and I have already started to dig the holes that will hold the posts for the chain-link fencing. Once that's in, I can move the dogs out here. Of course, there's still a lot of work, but it will get done." Eventually. He could only afford to pay the handyman for so long until more funds came in. Rubbing the back of his neck did little to relieve the instant tension. He needed at least six more hours a day to accomplish what he needed to do, and most of them had to be daylight hours. But God only provided them with a finite set of time, broken down by day, hour or minute, and he had to make it work within that time frame.

"Is there anything I can do to help?"

"As a matter of fact, there is." Ethan glanced down at Holly. He wanted to reach out and grab her hand, hold it and share this with her. Make her a more permanent part of his life and sanctuary. Whoa. He'd never had those thoughts before. Must be the idea that he'd just slipped another year closer to his mid-thirties. Besides, Holly was still in love with Jared, and any thoughts of getting involved with the single mom outside of helping with Cameron had to be stopped. He had to ignore the fact that his heart lightened when she was around and he enjoyed talking with her.

"I've seen what you've done with your shop and the mayor's Christmas decorations. I need some advice on how to decorate the foyer and office area downstairs as that will be what people see when they stop by."

"I can do that."

And yet, Ethan saw the hesitation in her eyes. He knew she was thinking about her store, her decorating business and spending time with Cameron. He also knew she felt she had a responsibility to him in order to make up for the rent she couldn't pay.

He didn't see it that way, but he'd already tripped over his words twice today and hurt her feelings. Trying to vocalize something when he couldn't formulate a valid sentence in his head wasn't worth it, either. The day he walked into her shop with Cameron in tow, he'd made the decision to let her remain through her busy season and try to rent it out after the new year.

Despite his financial needs, he still stood by that decision, even though it might cost him more in the long run, and he wasn't just thinking about money.

Chapter Seven

"Hi, Holly."

"Ethan." Holly's heart pounded when Ethan walked through the front door of 'Tis Always the Season. She didn't know if it was him or the pretty, petite blonde accompanying him that left her lungs out of oxygen and her stomach behaving as if there were a million butterflies trapped inside. Especially when the woman stood a tad bit closer to Ethan than Holly thought appropriate.

She knew a lot of people in town. The bottle blonde with the notepad and a more than casual interest in the shop remained a mystery. Holly stood behind the counter and gripped it tightly to keep from charging around the other side. "Is there something I can help you with?"

"Oh, no. I'm just here to look around and take some notes." She grabbed the pen clipped to the top of her notebook before flipping open the cover.

The woman's dismissal surprised her. So did the way Ethan placed his hand on the blonde's arm and gave her a guarded smile. More butterflies took flight. Funny, he never looked at Holly that way. Not that she wanted him to or anything like that, but what she interpreted as a protective gesture only reinforced the loneliness that crept up on her at the most inopportune times. Like now, for example. Forcing her mouth shut, Holly started to rearrange the Christmas-themed pens in the display canister. Santa needed to go next to Rudolph, not the snowman.

"Then let's get started. But first, I'd like to introduce you two. Beth, this is Holly. Holly, Beth."

"Pleased to meet you." Dropping the pen with the red package attached to the top next to the Christmas tree, Holly held her hand out to the woman, hoping her dislike didn't show. Ethan aside, she couldn't explain the sudden discomfort in Beth's presence. Maybe it was the freshly styled hair, the makeup or the perfect manicure. Or all three.

"Likewise." The woman's quick, limp grasp barely qualified as a handshake, her interest more in the man next to her. Beth's close-set eyes held a predatory gleam as she leaned closer to Ethan. The chill in the room did not come from the light breeze playing with the remaining leaves on the trees outside her front window.

Holly dropped her hand back on the counter and inhaled sharply, the woman's words finally registering in her brain. "Taking notes?"

"Yes." Her gaze flickered around the store, distaste etched in her perfectly made-up face. "I'm here to see about renting it once your lease is done at the end of the year. Now, Ethan, I don't have as much time as I'd like because of prior commitments, but please show me around."

A possible renter? Holly's spine fused into a straight rod. In all her preoccupation with Cam, closing shop and her new business, she hadn't even considered that Ethan would be showing the place while it was still occupied. But business was business, and she suspected he needed the money just like she did, especially after her visit to the permanent sanctuary outside of town yesterday and seeing how much Ethan had left to do.

She should be glad he had the opportunity to rent the place out with all the other spaces available in town, but her emotional side still resisted the idea that the shop had to close and she would give up on Jared's dream.

A dull pain spiderwebbed out from the base of her neck that even today's cranberry-scented candle couldn't alleviate. She refused to follow Ethan and Beth or hover anywhere near the couple. She didn't need to; she could hear almost every word the woman spoke, her loud cackle drowning out the Christmas music playing in the background.

"A Christmas shop? No wonder the place is going out of business."

Ethan's reply remained a mystery, but the woman's quick writing in her notebook worsened the pounding in Holly's skull. Not that she'd expect Ethan to defend her as a business owner, but she did as a friend, unless she'd totally misjudged him. After reaching in the top drawer for her bottle of pain relievers, Holly shoved two in her mouth and chased them down with this morning's warm water.

"And these colors and murals are awful. I presume I can paint the walls?"

Each word struck a dagger into Holly's heart, and she sank down into her chair. She and Jared had worked so hard painting the walls and deciding which murals they should do in the spirit of Christmas. Holly's favorite was the one of Santa standing next to the real fireplace on the opposite wall. Her gaze wandered to the small, framed picture she kept of her late husband by the cash register as she picked up the wooden ornament he'd carved for her.

The action brought her no comfort today. The shop was going away soon, and she'd be left with nothing but memories and heartache.

"Within reasonable guidelines. Of course, the cost will be yours. The lease only covers major issues, not cosmetic ones." The tone in Ethan's voice changed, and out of the corner of her eye, Holly watched him take a step to his right.

"And what about plumbing? I need at least three sinks." Beth placed her hand on Ethan's arm and squeezed gently, screaming high maintenance and territorial.

"You're welcome to change the interior to what you need, again at your own cost. However, the exterior and any signage have to be approved by the city historical society since this is listed as historical property." Holly detected another subtle change in Ethan's tone.

"Perfect. I don't suppose you know any plumbers, do you?"

Holly almost gagged at the woman's purr. If that was what men wanted these days, she was glad not to be out there dating. Her occasional loneliness didn't matter; she had friends. When she wanted to share a funny story or some other news, she had friends. If she needed to escape the confines of her home or store when Cam-

eron was out, she had friends. And now Ethan
had joined that rank, despite the occasional
closeness she felt around him or the weird sen-
sations inside her heart.

But date? She had no reason to date even if
that was what she wanted, which she didn't. She
had her hands full with her son, even though
things seemed to be turning around. Well, that
was until she saw his grades. The butterflies returned to her stomach. Their appointment with
the principal was in an hour.

"Plumbers? Not offhand, but I can ask around
for you." Ethan smiled at Beth again, but it died
quickly when he made eye contact with Holly.
Did she catch that look of desperation in his
eyes, or had she simply imagined it? Now he
looked quite content to be standing next to the
woman who wanted to be his future tenant.

Holly looked away first, rearranging the pens
again back to their original order, and wished
another customer would walk through the doors
and take her mind off Ethan and Beth.

No such luck. And there was only so much
she could do behind the counter.

"That would be perfect." Out of the corner of
her eye, Holly saw Beth move in a tad bit closer
to Ethan as she pulled a tape measure from her
purse. "Can you help me take some measure-

ments? I want to make sure that everything will work out to my specifications."

"Of course." But he didn't sound very happy about doing it.

After ten agonizing minutes of rearranging her sparse shelves and tree ornaments, Holly sighed in relief as the woman finally made a move to leave and take her cloying scent of expensive perfume, her notebook and her condescending attitude with her.

"Ethan, let's run over to the Sunrise Diner, grab a bite to eat and discuss all the details."

Ethan glanced at his watch and then back at Holly. His intense gaze pulled the air from her lungs. "I only have time for a cup of coffee. Holly and I have an appointment at one o'clock that we can't break."

"Thanks for your time, Mr. Buchanan." Ethan stood up and tugged at his collar, impatient to leave because he'd spent way too much times here in this very office. The man behind the desk had changed. He liked the slightly younger, more in-touch principal more than the old, strict one from his youth, but being in here brought back times he wasn't too proud of. Fortunately his neighbor, old man Witherspoon, had helped straighten him out, just like God had made sure

Ethan was now there to set Cameron on the right path.

"Yes, thank you." Holly stood up, as well.

"You're welcome." Mr. Buchanan stood and offered his hand to Holly and then to Ethan. "I'll be making an appointment to see Patrick's parents this afternoon and have a talk with all the teachers affected by the homework issue. If you have any other questions or concerns, you know where to find me."

"I do have one request." A smile tugged at Ethan's lips. Despite it all, he'd had some good times inside these walls.

"Sure. What is it?"

"I need to use a restroom."

"No problem. It's right across the hall. Just sign in at the front and get a visitor sticker." Mr. Buchanan leaned back in his chair and hid a grin behind his stern face. "But that's all. I can't allow you to roam the halls during school hours. It's against district policies. And behave, Mr. Pellegrino. Stories about the frogs in the cafeteria still circulate in these halls. It wouldn't be good to have to reprimand a Purple Heart recipient for misconduct, now, would it?"

"No, sir. Holly?" Heat crept to Ethan's cheeks as he helped Holly to her feet. He didn't realize that prank all those years ago would still echo in the conservatively painted brick walls.

"Frogs?" They left the principal's office. "Frogs? I don't think they have frog legs on the lunch menu."

"They don't. My friends and I let a bunch of frogs loose in the cafeteria the last day of school in eighth grade. We really didn't like the head lunch lady."

"And I'm letting you help with Cameron?" Holly's laughter belied her words.

Despite everything going on, her attitude had lightened over the past hour, and for a brief moment he wondered what it would be like if they were to go out and do something that wasn't related to Holly's business or the sanctuary or Cameron. Maybe they could attend another event like the Fall Harvest Festival or go to the movies.

Wrong. Because that would be a real date, something they agreed to do together, independent of what anyone else wanted or needed. He wasn't going to go there.

"Let's just say I had an intervention that summer." He signed them both in at the register on the front counter and handed her a visitor sticker. "I only had a few more problems after that."

"Which would be?"

Ethan held open the door leading into the hallway. Memories hit as soon as they stepped through. This time, though, the visit to the principal's office had gone much better than previous ones. "One of my old neighbors left his garage door open one day, so my friends and I took his motorized wheelchair out for a spin." Shame and remorse filled him. "It was fun, but we rode around so long, we ran the thing out of juice several blocks from the house and had to push it back."

"Sounds like you learned your lesson."

"More than that. When my mom found out, she marched me across the street to apologize and sign me up for free labor. I had to mow his yard that summer, rake his leaves in the fall and shovel his driveway in the winter." More memories filled him. "We actually bonded because of that incident, and Mr. Witherspoon ended up paying me a few bucks each time I helped him out, once he felt I paid for my crime. He was like another grandfather, one I could see on a daily basis." Ethan glanced up, wondering if Mr. Witherspoon could see him now. Because of his influence, he'd changed his life. Now Ethan had been given the chance to pay it back with Cameron and other boys in his position.

"He never had any children, so when he died, he left me a small inheritance. Enough to put the down payment on my house in town. I was also a pall bearer at his funeral."

Holly reached down and squeezed his right hand. "He sounds like a special person. I'm glad you had him in your life. And despite the frogs and the wheelchair and whatever else you did, I'm glad that you're in Cameron's life. These past few weeks have made me realize that he needs a man's influence."

Ethan tried to pull away, but Holly's grip remained strong. She held up his hand and smiled as she enclosed her other hand over his. Then she gently ran her fingers over the nubs.

His heartbeat quickened and moisture broke out on his forehead and under his arms. Unsure of what to say and needing an escape, Ethan spied the restroom sign. He needed to get away for a second. "Excuse me."

He opened the door, went inside and crossed the white tile floor to the sink. The cold water splashing against his face relieved some of his tension. He'd wanted Holly's acceptance, but now that he had it, he wasn't so sure it was a good thing. Or was it? *Okay, Lord, I'm trusting You on this one.*

Glancing up, an errant chuckle escaped his lips as he stared at the wads of dried toilet paper clinging to the ceiling. Things hadn't changed in here, but they were changing at an amazing speed in other areas. God was good.

Forty-five minutes later, Ethan let out a

whoop at the mailbox. Maybe things at the school hadn't changed over the years, but like the oncoming winter, he sensed a change in direction with the sanctuary and maybe, just maybe, with Holly. The sun seemed to shine brighter, and in his mind's eye, he could see the renovated barn clearly along with the brand-new fencing of the dog run. He inhaled the crisp scent of fall underlined with a hint of burning wood. "Thank you, Lord."

He pulled out the check for twenty thousand dollars from one of the prominent state representatives from Phoenix with a promise of yearly contributions. Meredith's letter campaign had worked. The retired military officer believed in the sanctuary. Believed in him.

Adrenaline surged through his veins, and he couldn't wait to get started. Things could only get better.

"Dear Lord, thank You for the food and drinks before us." Ethan's strong, unwavering voice drowned out the almost-muted professional football game playing on the television in the family room at Kristen's house Thanksgiving Day. "This table is full of Your abundant blessing. May all of us know that all good gifts come from You, and may each and every one of us serve Your heavenly will on a daily basis.

Thank You also for bringing family and friends together to share this day of Thanksgiving in Your loving presence. And bless those who are still overseas fighting for truth and freedom and especially for those and their families who have paid the ultimate sacrifice for their country. Amen."

Belief and hope in his voice mingled with a touch of sorrow as he squeezed Holly's hand. She did the same before she released his, knowing he thought about the men who had died beside him. "Amen."

"My turn," Kristen's daughter piped up from the children's table, a rectangular folding table placed next to the elegant dining table that sat the fourteen adults. "Rub-a-dub-dub, thanks for the grub. Yeah, God!"

Everyone laughed at Kira's words and began to pass the platters and bowls of food around.

Abundant blessings was right. Kristen had outdone herself again. Not only was the main table full of food and guests, there was also the children's table of eight, and the five teenagers and Cameron sat at the counter. Most of the people in attendance were family, but her friend always invited people with nowhere else to spend the holiday. With both Holly's parents gone now and then Jared, and the rest of her small family in Tucson, Holly now fell into that category.

But what was Ethan's story? He had family here. Even though he'd told her his mother went to Phoenix to be with her sister and he'd stayed behind because of the dogs, she knew there had to be others. So what story had Kristen concocted to get Ethan to sit by her side?

She grabbed the bowl of cranberry sauce and plopped some on her plate. When would her friend realize Holly wasn't interested in replacing Jared?

Or was she just fooling herself? Glancing out of the corner of her eye, she watched Ethan pour gravy on Kristen's grandmother's turkey and potatoes. The gentle way he treated the ninety-year-old woman endeared him to her and reminded her that there was more to him than he let on. He carried his scars on the inside, too. No doubt he had nightmares about the day that changed his life. They had that in common.

Two kindred souls, trying to make sense of the useless deaths while struggling to achieve a normalcy that always seemed beyond their grasp.

"Gravy?"

Holly's heart beat a bit faster as she caught his gaze. This time she saw him as a man, not a landlord or as someone helping her to keep Cameron in line. A man with hopes and dreams and feelings like she had. Catching her lip between her teeth, she nodded. "Yes, thank you."

"So tell us, Ethan, how does it feel to be back in Dynamite Creek after being on tour so long?" Kristen's husband, Tony, spoke from the head of the table.

Before Holly looked at Tony, she spied the tightness around Ethan's lips and sensed him stiffen. She knew firsthand he had a hard time talking about his time over there. In fact, outside the accident that took his fingers, he hadn't talked about Afghanistan at all. From the few articles she'd read online recently, most people didn't understand the returning vets or what it took to assimilate back into the general population, especially injured ones.

"It's good to be back. A little cold, but I'll get used to it again." The way he flexed his right hand made Holly wonder if it bothered him. If there weren't so many people around, she might have grabbed it and tried to massage some warmth back into it.

What was she thinking? Feeling the heat explode on her cheeks, she shoved some turkey into her mouth and chewed.

"It has been an unusually cold fall so far, and I can't believe how much snow we've gotten so early in the season. I can only hope that doesn't mean it's going to be a horrible winter.

Now, who needs more cranberry sauce?" As if sensing his discomfort, Kristen held up a small white serving bowl.

"I imagine it gets pretty hot over in Afghanistan. Kind of like Yuma or Lake Havasu on a bad July day. And wearing all that gear and being away from family, that's gotta be tough." Tony kept talking, even after Holly saw Kristen poke him in the stomach.

"You know, I just don't understand this war or why our men and women are over there. Now, World War II, that made sense." Kristen's grandmother spoke up. "Why are we there again? The deaths, the violence, it seems so senseless. I can't watch the news about it anymore."

"I know what you mean, Nana," Kristen's cousin said from the other end of the table.

Ethan tensed even more, and Holly saw him struggle to not jump from his seat and storm out the door. Before the conversation spiraled out of control, Holly placed her hand on his arm, squeezed gently and stared into the old woman's faded blue eyes before she made eye contact with everyone at the table. "We're there to defend freedom. Something this country was founded on. Something we shouldn't forget."

"You're right. Nana, we should all be thankful for our military and all that Ethan and his fellow soldiers have done and sacrificed for our freedom," Tony said.

When everyone at the table voiced their agreement, Ethan's muscles relaxed, yet the tranquil mood of the day had changed.

"Did you know Ethan's building a dog sanctuary outside of town for our service men and women who don't have anywhere for their pets to go while they're away?" Holly pursued a neutral topic.

"And I'm helping out," Cameron announced from the counter. Holly saw him puff up with pride, and it gladdened her to see him so interested in something. Her heart stalled for a moment. Or was it the attention he received from Ethan? Attention that he hadn't been getting from her because of her preoccupation with the shop? "I get to feed and play with the dogs, and when the sanctuary is fully operational, I'm going to be on the staff. Isn't that right, Mr. P.?"

Those weren't the exact words Ethan had said to Cameron, but the boy had been a big help to him, and he liked having him around. He liked having Holly around, too. She helped drive away his loneliness and made his nightmares recede. She brought him hope.

Ethan caught her gaze. He hadn't had a chance to mention his more permanent solution to her yet because of timing issues, but that had to change. Holly's stunned expression told him she wasn't particularly happy about it, and he couldn't blame her. Again he'd overstepped his boundaries with Cameron. "With your mother's permission, of course."

"Mom?"

"We'll discuss this later, okay?" Holly hid behind a wall of hair as she stabbed at her pile of mashed potatoes. Gravy slid out of the gash she'd put in the side and spilled into her green beans, but she didn't seem to notice.

"Okay." Holly's son wasn't pleased with the answer.

"Dogs?" Kristen's grandmother spoke up next to him. "I like dogs. Always have. Too bad my Fred was allergic to them. Maybe I should get one."

"Nana, I bet Ethan would be happy to bring a few into the nursing home for a visit." Kristen broke in, saving Ethan from a reply.

"That's a great idea. I've heard stories of how animals, dogs in particular, are good for the emotions of the elderly and shut-ins," the woman he identified as Kristen's sister Kate piped in. "I bet the dogs are lonely without their owners. No offense, Ethan, I'm sure you take really good care of them, but it could be beneficial for all of them."

"None taken." He acknowledged the blonde

before his attention returned to Holly. Having Cameron and even Holly at times helping with the dogs had been helpful for all of them, too. He liked their company, and if he wasn't mistaken, they liked his, as well. Their gazes caught as she looked up from her plate and gave him a half smile, but it was the compassion written in her eyes that made his pulse accelerate.

"Dogs are good for everyone." Her hand covered his and she squeezed gently. For a moment, he forgot about the others gathered in the room, the food, the football game in the background and the nightmares from Afghanistan. The warmth of her touch before she pulled away put hope in his heart.

"I'll speak with the manager when we drop Nana off tonight." Tony's words broke the connection.

"So is that all you're doing, then? I'd heard Pastor Matt was trying to recruit you as the youth pastor for our church," Kristen's father said from the other end of the table.

Ethan shook his head to clear away the lingering effects of Holly's gaze. He had to focus on the here and now, not on the woman who carried around the same amount of emotional baggage as he did. "He's trying, but I've got another idea in mind." He eyed Holly's son but remained silent. If these people didn't know of Cameron's troubles, he wasn't about to be the one to tell them. "I'm also working with another organization to rescue abused dogs, get them out of Afghanistan and reunite them with the men who'd adopted them but then got shipped home."

"Interesting. You hear so much about the poor people over there, but you never really hear about much else. I guess they would have dogs just like the rest of us." Kate scooped out more mashed potatoes onto her plate and held up the bowl. "Anyone else?"

"I'm good, thank you. Yes, they do have dogs and cats but unfortunately, they don't think about them in the same way we do." Ethan wiped his mouth and stared at his empty plate, thinking about Scooter, the yellow mutt that had strayed into camp one night, bloodied and battered from abuse. His appetite disappeared. The dog had ended up losing his mangled leg and one eye, and as far as he knew, Scooter was still in that base camp. Ethan expected a phone call any day requesting his services to help bring Scooter stateside.

The redhead he recognized as Stephanie with the twin girls spoke up from the far end of the table. "Finding the funding and supplies must be a challenge." She turned to her daughters. "Girls, quit fidgeting. You may be excused, but take your plates to the kitchen first."

"It has been. But I've been praying a lot and sending out a lot of letters. I'm finally finding support." Like a moth drawn to light, his gaze sought out Holly's. He wanted to reach for her hand and feel the connection, feel complete, but her attention was focused on her son.

"Praise be to God. It's important for our men and women to know their pets are safe while they're away." Kristen's mother, Hannah, broke in and began to pile the empty dinner plates. "Keep doing what the good Lord is telling you to do. Everything will fall into place. You'll see."

Kate's husband, Cory, snapped his fingers and pointed at Ethan. "I know the general manager of that pet-food chain store. Sometimes he gets in broken or damaged bags of food and doesn't know what to do with them. I'll make sure he has your name." He pushed back his chair and patted his belly. "Another wonderful meal, Kristen. Thanks for putting up with us again this year."

"No problem. I love having you. All of you." At her direct stare, Ethan shifted in his seat. "Does anyone need anything else?"

"No, dear. Boys?" She motioned for the teenagers to step forward. "Start clearing the table, please. Ethan, we sometimes get donations that aren't quite resalable at the church thrift shop.

I'll make sure to save all the towels and blankets for you," Hannah announced, daring anyone to refute her.

Despite the noise and activity, Ethan sat there stunned. God continued to answer his prayers each and every day with the generosity being bestowed upon him. *Let go, let God.*

He had, or at least was trying to, and things were starting to fall into place. This time he caught and held Holly's gaze. But would He answer Ethan's other prayer? The one with the mixed-up feelings about the woman beside him that he had a hard time putting words to?

"Ethan likes you." Kristen handed her a rinsed plate.

Denial sprung to Holly's lips, but she couldn't force the words out. Something had changed between her and Ethan over the past few weeks, even today, and it frightened her. Entertaining any type of romantic ideas with her soon-to-be former landlord was out of the question. Holly's hand shook as she set the plate in the dishwasher in front of the last one she'd put in. "We're almost out of room here. We'll have to do the rest by hand."

"Quit changing the subject. He likes you. You know it and you're running scared."

"He's just being friendly and helping out

with Cameron," she retorted a bit defensively. There, she'd said it. The truth. So why did it hurt? Could Holly be a tad bit jealous of her son because of the attention Ethan was giving him? Nonsense. She only had platonic feelings for the man.

Ethan and Tony brought in another stack of dishes from the other room and set them on the counter. How many more dishes were there? And they hadn't even started on the pots and pans yet. Holly let out a groan, but she wouldn't trade Thanksgiving at Kristen's for anything. Now she knew how the turkey felt, though, before her friend had put it in the oven. Full didn't even compute in her brain.

"Almost done in there?" Ethan grinned at her before he turned away and headed back out the door.

Why had the air just disappeared from her lungs?

"Really?" Kristen rinsed off another plate. "I see the way he looks at you. And I see the way you look at him."

"We're just friends," Holly protested. Maybe a bit too much by the looks of things. Kristen's eyebrows almost touched her bangs.

"Right." A smile split Kristen's face. "You've got it all wrong and you're lying to yourself. I can see you're interested. He's a good man. I think you should give him a chance."

Holly's fingers tightened around the plate until her knuckles turned white. Anger, denial, fractured by her confused feelings about Ethan, punctured her thoughts. "I'm not interested in replacing Jared, Kristen, and you know that. He was the love of my life."

Kristen sighed and grabbed the dish towel from the counter to dry her hands. Then she placed them on Holly's shoulders and squeezed gently. A frown furrowed her brows and concern laced her voice. "Holly, I know this is hard, especially around the holidays, but Jared is dead. He's not coming back and you know it. You've got to move on."

"Is it time for dessert yet?" Kristen's niece, Molly, stuck her head through the kitchen door.

Without missing a beat, Kristen grabbed a pitcher and handed it to the ten-year-old. "Not yet, but if you help us out, we may get done that much sooner and then it will be time. Why don't you empty all the water glasses and then water my plants on the back porch? And when that's done, we'll be that much closer."

Holly's reprieve ended when the girl sped from the room, full pitcher in hand. Despite having eaten too much of Kristen's good food, butterflies still managed to find room inside.

She had to straighten out her friend once and for all. "Look. I know you mean well, but when I'm ready, you'll be the first to know, okay?"

"You're never going to be ready. I know you. Hiding away and sitting home alone, focusing on Cameron or work, isn't the answer."

"But I promised Jared that I would love him forever."

As Kristen scrubbed at the large turkey pan, water sloshed out of the sink. "And you will. He was your husband and Cameron's father. Did anything Pastor Matt say last Sunday sink in? Our physical hearts may not be that big, but God gave our emotional hearts enough room to love many times over. I love my children. I love Tony. I love my parents even though they drive me crazy most of the time. I love you like a sister, which is why I'm being so hard on you. God has given you the ability to love a lot. He's given you room. It's up to you to decide what to do with it. Live again, Holly. It's what Jared would have wanted. If the roles had been reversed and you had died, wouldn't you have wanted Jared to find happiness again?"

"But—"

Kristen held up a soapy hand. "Don't answer. Just think about it."

Holly fell silent. What could she say? Kristen didn't understand. None of her friends did. They still had their spouses, their happily-ever-afters. They didn't know the pain of waking up in an empty bed and reaching out to feel the warmth but only finding cold sheets. They hadn't experienced the loneliness of not being able to share news of their day, the loss of security or the hardship of raising a child by themselves.

Looking out the window over the sink, Holly watched Ethan play football with a few of the other men and the teenage boys. Cameron's face lit up with the attention. She swallowed and held back her tears. Her son deserved so much more than she could give him.

"Ethan's a good man. Look at the way he interacts with Cameron and the other kids. Don't you think God might be taking an active role in this by bringing two lonely people together? Things don't happen by coincidence. There's always a bigger plan. We might not understand it at the time, but eventually we will. On His time and terms."

Finished with scrubbing the turkey pan, Kristen rinsed it and handed it to Holly to dry. "Hello? Anyone home? I know you're here because I see you, but I don't think you're really *here*. You always seem to withdraw at the mention of God lately. He hasn't forsaken you."

"Some days it feels like He has."

"He hasn't." Kristen pulled her hands from

the soapy water and wiped them on her apron before she put her arms around Holly's shoulders and squeezed. "As a parent you know you have to let your child or children live their own lives and learn from their mistakes as well as their triumphs. As our Heavenly Father, God allows us to do the same, but He is always there when we need Him. Now, back to Ethan. Take a good look at him and open your heart to the possibilities."

Through misty eyes, Holly continued to stare out the window. Maybe Kristen was right. Maybe it was time to let go of her past and live again. And possibly love. In only a few years, Cameron would be grown and off to college and Holly would be by herself. Lonely and alone. Is that what she wanted? Yes—no— maybe not, but could she allow herself to open her heart again?

Chapter Eight

Ethan's first Thanksgiving back on American soil was turning out to be a good one—aside from the mention of Afghanistan over dinner. Great food, great company, and his favorite football team had won by scoring a field goal in overtime. Kristen's family had come up with solutions to some of his needs at the sanctuary, and something had shifted between him and Holly. God was on his team.

Winded from the physical activity of playing football with the guys, he leaned over, placed his hands on his knees and tried to catch his breath. He smiled at Holly as she looked at him through the kitchen window. Her serious expression put him on edge. He broke the contact and glanced in Cameron's direction and saw her son approaching with a basketball. Everything was good there. A quick surveillance of the rest of the yard reassured him that nothing seemed out of the ordinary. Something was wrong, but he had no clue as to its origins. Sometimes he just couldn't figure women out.

"Can I ask you something, Mr. P.?" Cameron motioned him away from the other people in the backyard.

"Sure." He glanced at the window again, but Holly had disappeared. Ethan righted himself and they headed toward the shed, where Tony had hung a basketball hoop.

Cameron took a shot, but the ball hit the backboard and dropped to the ground. Ethan retrieved the ball and bounced it between his two hands before he lobbed it into the air. The sensation felt strange at first, but he realized he didn't need all his fingers to shoot a basket. The ball rimmed the hoop and dropped in.

Cameron retrieved the ball, took another shot and missed.

Ethan knew what he was going to do with the open spot next to the barn where the cement had already been laid. "Next time you're at the farm, I'll teach you how to shoot. I don't think we have time today."

Cameron missed another basket.

Ethan retrieved the ball again and lobbed it back to Cameron. "You're not concentrating. What's bugging you?"

"I don't know." He dribbled the ball with more force than necessary. "School. Everything. My mom."

At the mention of Holly, the Thanksgiving meal became lead in his stomach. She had been rather distracted lately, and even today her attention had wandered during the meal. Her serious expression a few minutes ago bothered him more than it should. Was there something else wrong? "What's up with your mom?"

"I know she's lonely. She doesn't laugh anymore, and all she does is work. I wish she'd be happy again. Like she used to be."

"What do you mean?" Ethan lunged for the ball before it slipped past him. Cameron's aim needed work. This time, instead of giving the ball back to Holly's son, he dribbled it himself, the steady beat keeping rhythm with his heart.

"She was always singing and laughing, and she told the most amazing jokes. She was always smiling and cooking and there for me— it's just different now. I want my old mom back."

"It can be tough. Losing someone you love can be very difficult, and everyone has a different grieving period. It takes longer for some than others." The ball smacked against his palm until Ethan trapped it. He wasn't in the mood to play basketball anymore and sensed the moment had passed for Cameron, too.

"But it's been so long." Cameron fisted his hands. "Sometimes I don't feel like I exist anymore. That she doesn't care."

Ethan digested his words. "She loves you very much, Cameron. That's why she works all the time. To make sure you have what you need. But I think there's something else that's bothering you. What is it? Maybe I can help."

The boy kicked at some gravel littering the court. "I want another dad. Someone like you." The color drained from the boy's face. "I mean, I loved my real dad. Is it wrong that I want another one?"

Ethan's heart contracted. If God had given him a son, he would have wanted him to be just like Cameron. While Ethan didn't know what was in store for his future, he knew that somehow Cameron was involved. So were other boys at risk. He'd tucked away the idea of Pastor Matt's Sunday sermon on hearts and loving for future reference but hadn't thought he'd need it so soon. "I think God made our hearts so big so we could love lots of people that come in and out of our lives. Your dad will always have a special place there that no one can compete with, but there's a lot more room."

"Do you think my mom's heart is big enough?"

Was it? Ethan had to choose his words carefully. He couldn't speak for Holly. "I think your mom needs more time. When you love someone and have them taken away from you, there's a healing process that needs to happen. She might not be ready yet." Despite the late-afternoon sunshine, his day dimmed. Holly affected him more than he liked to admit.

"Will she ever be?"

"That's up to her."

Kristen rang the bell hanging from the back porch. "Dessert time. Last one in gets nothing but crust."

"I'll race you." Cameron sprinted away before Ethan could react.

He let Holly's son win, not because the boy was younger, but because Ethan was digesting the words he'd spoken to Cameron. He couldn't deny any longer that he had feelings for Holly. He just hoped his advice worked not only on Cameron, but for himself, as well.

"Can you help me make something for my mom for Christmas?" Cameron turned away from Bear's kennel after he finished feeding the dog the day after Thanksgiving.

"What did you have in mind?" The idea that Cameron had come to him for help lightened Ethan's mood, yet concerned him because of the boy's growing attachment. Despite the positive interest from Kristen's family members and friends yesterday, another rejection for funds for the sanctuary had turned the promising day into one filled with more questions than answers. Sure, the check he'd already received was enough to complete the renovations on the barn and get the dog run ready, but he still needed food and supplies. The community was willing to chip in, but even their resources wouldn't be enough in the long run.

Was he doing the right thing? He'd made a mistake in judgment before and it had cost five people their lives. He'd misjudged some of Cameron's actions, like at the Fall Festival when he'd caught the boys smoking. Yet the boy had turned around, and something in Cameron's eyes today made Ethan think that all was not lost. He had to let go of the past and remember that God was in charge and that things came about on His time, not Ethan's. Things happened for a reason. Just the idea that he was brought into Cameron's life when he seemed to need Ethan the most was something he couldn't ignore.

"My dad had a shop in the shed behind our house. I used to go in there and watch him work sometimes. I want to use his tools to make something for her, but he always told me never to use any of them by myself. Obviously, I can't ask my mom."

Right. Jared had always talked about having his own woodworking shop one day, and he was glad that Cameron's dad had made that dream come true before his untimely death. Jared would be happy to know that his son showed an interest in learning how to use his tools, and Holly shouldn't mind because she hadn't disposed of them, so she was probably saving them for Cameron when he got older. "Sure thing. How about if we do it on Saturday while your mom's at the store?"

Holly heard the sound of power tools and voices coming from the large shed in her backyard when she stepped from her car. Not just any voices, but Ethan's and Cameron's. Normally she didn't come home for lunch, but today she'd forgotten to bring the small gift for the baby shower that she was attending this afternoon, which left her no choice.

Awareness of where Ethan and her son were punched her in the stomach and left her nerves raw and exposed. Jared's woodworking shop was inside. She hadn't been in there since her husband's death. She couldn't face it. Her fingers clenched her purse strap and all moisture fled her mouth as she slowly crossed the yard. The open door beckoned, and drawn to it, she couldn't refuse where her feet took her.

Guilt over the accident and the memories of Jared inside the shop were more than she could handle. Pain tore through her, ripping apart any thread of composure she had left.

Today of all days was the anniversary of Jared's and Olivia's deaths.

Tears poured down her face as her fingers gripped the threshold, the scent of cut wood filling her nose as she peeked inside. Nausea hit her hard. The aroma that she used to love made her tears flow faster. Through the haze, she spotted Cameron and Ethan bent over the workbench working on a cut piece of wood. She still couldn't face it. "No."

She barely heard her whisper or the guttural moan as she pushed herself away and stumbled backward. Her purse dropped to the ground right before her knees sank into the dead grass. Wrapping her arms around her middle, she curled up into a quivering mass of emotion. Her fingers squeezed her sides as if trying to release the blackness consuming her from the inside.

"Mom?" She heard Cam's voice as if coming through a fog.

"Holly? What's wrong?" Within seconds, Ethan was at her side.

"What are you doing in there?" Holly glanced up just in time to catch the stricken look on her son's face. She tried to reach out but her arm dropped to her waist.

"We— Nothing." Cameron shrank before her eyes. Her inability to control her fragile emotions had hurt her son. Moisture burned the back of her eyes again. The person she loved and who meant the whole world to her now had retreated back into the shed.

"Cam, wait." Holly swatted at her tears, stood and stumbled after him. Once inside, she rubbed her eyes, trying to regain her composure. Her chin trembled as she inhaled a shaky breath and looked at her son standing behind the workbench where Jared used to make his masterpieces. How tall and proud he stood and seemingly so grown-up. She bit her bottom lip and tapped her hands against her mouth, fresh tears lingering in her eyes. Her pain refused to subside. Sawdust littered her son's hair and stuck to his cheeks and chin. With a watery smile, she dusted them off as she used to do with Jared. The memory blazed another trail of tears down her cheeks. "I'm sorry. I— It's— just—this was your father's place. I—I'm having a hard time, that's all."

Through a haze, her gaze swept across the small interior, and she remembered the love that Jared had put into making that space his refuge. Shelves lined the walls, the cubbies and holders filled with every tool imaginable. He'd even built his own movable bases so that his saws and other necessary items could be positioned where he needed them. Countertops hid more drawers until every space in the area had been utilized to its fullest capacity.

"I used to love sitting in here with your father, watching him make his creations."

"Mr. P. is helping me make something, but I can't show you just yet."

Jared had been the same way when he was making a gift for her. Like father, like son. Her lip trembled and her legs lost the ability to hold her weight. She collapsed onto the stool in the corner and buried her head in her hands. She knew she should have disposed of everything, yet she couldn't. Not then, not now, even though the money she could sell it for would pay for quite a few things.

It would be like giving Jared up again.

Kristen was wrong. Pastor Matt was wrong. She couldn't do it. She couldn't give up her dead husband like that and make room for someone else. Her heart wasn't that big. She wouldn't replace him despite her loneliness or any other emotion that snuck up on her.

She heard Ethan shift in the doorway. He'd only been trying to help her son, but he'd unknowingly entered a place that he didn't belong.

She couldn't bear it. Not today. Not any day. She still felt Jared here as strongly as she did days before the accident. This spot was off-limits. It had to remain Jared's. She glanced from her son to Ethan and then back. "I don't want you in here, Cam. You, either, Ethan."

"But, Mom." Hurt and anger laced his expression. "You ruin everything." Cam fled from the shed.

Holly stumbled from the stool and heard it clatter behind her. She tried to squeeze past Ethan, but he held her in place. "Holly, please. I'll take the blame. I won't come back in here, but don't do this to Cameron. This was his father's stuff. He should be using it. It's what Jared would have wanted. Jared is dead. Despite how much you want it, or how much I want those five people in Afghanistan to come back, it's not going to happen."

He lifted his hand as if to touch her face but let it drop loosely to his side. More words hovered on his lips, but no sound came out. In his expression, she saw her own horrors and found herself in his arms.

She did know that, but it still didn't make it right. All she knew was that she needed to allow herself to grieve and work through Jared's death, but she couldn't. Not with the knowledge she held inside her. Clinging to Ethan's shirt, her fingers clawed at the flannel fabric. His warm embrace cocooned her, made her feel almost complete again, which confused her even more. Tears spilled down her cheeks and saturated the red-checked cloth as she tried to purge herself and let go. "I still don't understand. Why did he have to die on me?"

"I don't have an answer for that. Only God does." Ethan's fingers rubbed the small of her back, trying to massage away her pain. It felt right holding her in his arms, right to lean his cheek against the crown of her head, right to whisper words of encouragement and forgiveness in the still air around them.

She raised her head, her eyes full of tears and a remorse that sucker-punched him in the gut. There was no denying it now. Somewhere, somehow, he'd fallen for Jared's widow.

"I was driving that night. I killed him."

He stiffened at her words and understood the responsibility weighing on her. They both had been put in positions that had resulted in horrible outcomes. The nightmares of what happened in Afghanistan hadn't decreased, and each night the images of his friends and colleagues, their faces frozen in motion at the time of the blast, lingered in the deep recesses of his brain. What images of that night tortured Holly? Could he make them go away?

"It wasn't anyone's fault. Quit beating your-self up over what can't be changed." He should listen to his own advice.

He stared down at Holly's tearstained face, sensed her vulnerability and her despair. It matched his own. Two lonely people, strug-gling with the knowledge that their actions had caused other people to lose their lives. It was a heavy guilt to bear. After wiping the tears from her cheeks, his hands cupped the sides of her face.

In a trance, he leaned down and gently kissed her lips, as if he could wipe away the pain of her loss and maybe lose some of it himself. He had to let her know she wasn't alone anymore, unable to share her burden. He deepened the kiss, trying to purge not only her memories but his own, as well. His heart pounded, crashing against his rib cage, unused to his reaction to Holly. She made him feel alive again. Whole. Ready to let go of his past and embrace what-ever the future held in store for him.

Holly trembled and returned his touch, her soft gasps encouraging him to deepen the embrace. Her fingers laced through his hair, pulling him closer. It all felt so right, holding her, kissing her, creating a new bond between them that had nothing to do with Cameron. His heart lightened.

A few moments later, she stiffened and pulled away, her fingers covering her lips. Her flush disappeared, the white a contrast to the dark wood-stained shelves lining the walls. More tears filled her eyes, twisting his gut so that it resembled the mass of wood shavings piled on the floor. "No, I can't do this. Just go. Go away and leave me alone."

"I'm sorry. I didn't mean for that to happen." But was he really sorry? He'd be lying if he said that the kiss had no effect on him, because it was more than just a physical reaction. Confusion coiled inside him like a snake ready to strike. What he'd just done was wrong, and Holly was paying the price.

"I am sorry, Holly. I'll go now." Ethan scraped his fingers through his hair, his voice scratchy with emotion and remorse. The last thing he'd wanted to do was hurt her. He'd overstepped his bounds. In the shadows clinging to the back corners of the shop, voiceless faces stared back at him: Jared, the pastor, his men, and the woman and child he should have protected. Until both he and Holly could come to terms with their loss, neither one was free to move on.

After Ethan left the shed, Holly sank to the floor, a sob managing to escape from her throat. What had just happened? Ethan had kissed her, and she'd kissed him back. She'd done nothing to stop him, instead encouraging him to deepen the embrace. She'd kissed another man. Kristen would be happy. Holly was miserable.

And it wasn't because she didn't enjoy it. It was because she did.

She'd ignored her promise to Jared.

She fingered the wooden whistle attached to her key chain that Jared had carved for her their first Christmas together. The anniversary of his death, the death of their dream and their second child, hung heavily in the air.

Would she ever find peace or forgiveness?

Lord, I'm so confused. I don't understand what You want from me. What is Your will? What do I need to do?

Only silence surrounded her in the warm, almost suffocating air. *Answer me. Please.*

No response, but what had she really expected? God hadn't answered her in her darkest hours after Jared's death or her miscarriage. He didn't answer her now, which made her struggle. If God existed, why did He allow such pain and suffering? Why did He call some people home and leave others behind? Yet how could she account for the miracle of birth or the beauty surrounding her? Or how sometimes in the stillness of the morning and again at night she could almost feel a comforting presence wrapping around her? But why didn't He answer now when she needed Him?

More pain sliced through her midsection, making her relive the agony of that night in the hospital. She'd known her husband was dead, that she'd killed him, and that she'd also killed their unborn child, Olivia.

More alone than ever, Holly pulled herself up off the floor, stumbled to the door and across the brown grass to the back porch. From her vantage point, she could see that only her car was parked in the driveway. A momentary relief filled her. Ethan had left, but had he taken Cam with him?

Cameron. He'd never seen that emotional side to her before because she'd always managed to hide it behind closed doors. Her nails dug into her palms and her teeth worried her bottom lip. A different anxiety emerged. The back door banged open when she pushed on it. The loud thump resounded in the dim kitchen. "Cameron?"

No answer.

She sped through the house searching for her son, even going as far as to look under his bed. Only Figaro's golden eyes stared back at her. Sitting back on her heels, she grabbed her cell phone and dialed Ethan, tapping her foot impatiently until he picked up on the third ring. "Is Cameron with you?"

"He is. I figured you needed some time."

Holly clutched the phone. "Thanks."

"Would you like to talk to him? Here."

Holly heard Ethan transfer the phone. Soon her son's breathing filled her ear, but no words accompanied it. Her stomach clenched and pain stabbed her behind her eyes. She'd messed up big-time and her son had paid the price. More emotion covered her like an unwelcome blanket. "I'm so sorry, Cam. I overreacted. We'll talk about it later, okay? I love you."

It took him a few heartbeats to respond. "I love you more."

"I love you most. I'll see you at five, okay?"

"Bye, Mom." He disconnected the phone.

"Bye, Cam. I'm so sorry." Her words shattered the stillness inside the room. Cameron had been terrified by her reaction. All he'd wanted to do was make something with his father's tools. He had every right to. She grabbed a T-shirt lying outside the hamper and pressed it against her face.

Ethan was right. It was what Jared would have wanted. But maybe it wasn't that her son was using the tools, but Ethan himself.

He'd made himself a part of their lives, first by helping out with Cameron and then by kissing Holly. Her fear grew. Ethan was taking over Jared's place. She tried to picture her late husband in her mind's eye, but Ethan's face surfaced. Wiping away her tears blurred the image like a Picasso, but the pieces remained even after she opened her eyes and dropped Cameron's shirt into the hamper.

She'd get through this. She had to.

More shadows crept into Cameron's room. Holly walked to the window and gazed outside. The dark clouds emerging from the west matched her mood. There'd been no snow predicted today. Sweat slicked her clenched fists. Maybe she should cancel attending the baby shower and reschedule her appointment with Abby to talk about setting up the Christmas decorations at the bed-and-breakfast. Ethan could bring Cam home and then she could hibernate and take care of some things around the house. No. Her head battled with her emotions. She needed the company of her girlfriends right now and the money that another decorating job would bring in.

Fear would not win.

"Hi, Holly. It's so good to see you again. Come on in." Abby Preston ushered her into the renovated foyer inside the old Victorian bed-and-breakfast she owned and gave her a hug.

Holly returned the embrace. "You, too, Abby."

"Thanks for coming on such short notice. It'll be nice to catch up, though." Abby directed her into the empty parlor, their shoes clicking against the tile and then the wood floor. A hint of spiced apple drifted through the air from the candle burning on the fireplace mantel.

"Definitely. I wish we had more time to chat at those chamber mixers, but there are always so many distractions." Holly settled herself on the frosted blue fleur-de-lis, Queen Ann–style chair. Despite her anxiety of going to the monthly gatherings, Holly knew that she needed to make an appearance every so often to keep up on what happened around Dynamite Creek.

"I know. When I first moved here, I knew no one. Now I don't seem to have a moment's peace." Yet from the smile on the blonde's face as she took a seat on the matching sofa, Holly guessed it didn't bother her a bit.

Holly's fingers ran along the ornately carved chair arms as her gaze flitted around the cozy room spruced in a blue-and-gold theme, mixed with antiques and time-period replicas. She imagined the small Christmas tree in the corner filled with cherubs and bows and garland draped over the heavy, full-length curtains and fireplace.

"That's Dynamite Creek for you." Sometimes

the town wasn't very welcoming to outsiders. Holly had grown up in Flagstaff, but the town had welcomed her with open arms because of Jared.

Despite her California background, Abby had no trouble fitting in, and it wasn't just because she was related to one of the original founding families. Her husband, Cole, a local, had had a harder time because of some bad business dealings, but he had managed to work things out. Now he and his partner, Robert, had a booming business in renovating the older houses in town, which was probably why Holly was here to talk about Abby's Christmas decorating for the Bancroft Bed & Breakfast.

"I know." Her laughter filled the area. "Would you like some coffee and a slice of banana bread? Mrs. Wendt brought it by earlier."

"I'm fine, thanks. Maybe I'll take a slice to go."

"You'd think by osmosis I'd learn how to bake, living with Cole and wedged between the two prize-winning bakers in town, but that's just not the case. It still bothers me that Cole is a better cook than I am, but then again I don't have to spend much time in the kitchen and can mingle with our guests."

"Which you're good at. And trust me, having a man who knows his way around the kitchen is a good thing. Especially toward the end." Beside her, Abby shifted, her belly starting to protrude with her first child. The woman had blossomed the past few months in more ways than one.

"Yeah, I've heard I'm in for a fun time. Pretty soon I won't be able to see my feet and Cole will have to paint my toenails for me."

"But it's all worth it. You forget about everything, even the pain, when the doctor places your baby in your arms for the first time." The joy, the happiness, the intense emotion of love and protectiveness. The bond created by sharing the experience. Her fingers curled into fists. *Stop it. Stop going there.* This was Abby's moment. The woman, like most of the town, knew nothing of Holly's miscarriage after the accident, and now was not the time to mention it. "Have you had any cravings yet?"

"Bacon and soup of all things. Are you okay?" Concern laced Abby's brow.

"I'm fine. Really. Just a bit tired, that's all."

"And why wouldn't you be? Running two businesses all by yourself and raising your son. I know I couldn't do it alone. I'm so blessed to have Cole." Abby's hands flew to her cheeks, but Holly could still see the redness underneath. "Oh, Holly. I'm so sorry."

"It's okay, Abby. That's life." Holly had found her true love, but he'd been taken away from her.

Would she find happiness again if she wanted to? Ethan's face intruded into her thoughts again and she remembered the feel of his lips on hers along with all the emotions behind the caress. It was all Holly could do not to cover her mouth. She pushed all the memories away.

Despite Holly's recent thoughts of how she missed being in a relationship, Jared had been the love of her life and she had no plans to replace him. She couldn't go through the pain if she allowed herself to fall in love again and something happened to him, too.

"Now, let's see what you want me to do and I'll give you a quote."

A look of relief crossed Abby's features at the change in conversation. She stood and headed back toward the double doors. "Your flyer came at just the right time, you know. I wasn't sure how I'd get this place decorated for the holidays. We're just so busy these days, and I don't quite have the energy I used to, if you know what I mean. This is one of the rooms on the list, of course the living room is where the main focus would be."

"I do, and that's why I'm here." This was Holly's second potential big Christmas decorating job, and she'd do better to focus on that instead of Ethan. She stared at the large living room and fell in love with the architecture in here, too. "You've done an amazing job of reno-vating the interior and bringing it back to its for-mer glory. I can see a twelve-foot Christmas tree in the corner, decorated with Victorian-style bows and ornaments. Garland strung across the windows and doorways and a wreath over the fireplace. What colors do you want to use?"

"I don't know. Surprise me. You'll have to wrap garland around the staircase banisters and deck out the dining room, as well."

"Of course, and I envision red and white poinsettias in the dining room. What about the guest rooms?"

Abby put her hands on her back and stretched. "If you have the time and we don't go over bud-get, I'd like to see something on a much smaller scale done in there, too. At least some kind of centerpiece for the dressers and maybe some garlands—oh, and wreaths in every front win-dow."

Holly remembered the days of an achy back and equally sore feet. Which reminded her again that it was a small price to pay for the miracle of birth and holding an infant in your arms for the first time. This time when tears threatened, Holly managed to keep them at bay. She would not break down again. "What type of decora-tions do you have?"

"Not much but the exterior lighting, which

Cole and Robert have promised to put up tomorrow. Most of what my grandparents left behind was old and didn't fit the theme I have in mind."

"May I see them? I might be able to save you some money by incorporating what you already have with other things and create something new. If anything, they can be used in the guest rooms if the colors don't match."

"That would be awesome. They're in the old garage out back. We can load them in your car and you can take them with you. If they don't work for me, maybe they will for someone else. Or you can donate them to charity."

Twenty minutes and a trunkful later, Holly accepted a slice of banana bread. "Okay, then, let me get to work on it. I'll get back to you tonight if possible with the proposal."

Abby put her hand on Holly's arm and squeezed gently. "Holly, you're hired. I have three thousand dollars to work with. I have faith that you'll be able to make this place a showcase and get more customers in the process. I need it up by next weekend, though. Is that going to be a problem?"

"Not at all." She thought of her schedule and currently pending commitments. Who needed sleep? Of course, with her schedule filling up so fast, she was going to have to rely on Kristen to help out with Cameron on the nights she couldn't be home. There was only so much she could do while she worked at the shop. Maybe she should just close down and be done with it. Turmoil reduced her to tears and she walked quickly to her car. She wanted to hold on to her late husband's dream as long as she could, because once it was over, she'd have to finally say goodbye to Jared.

Chapter Nine

"**P**astor Matt, can I talk to you for a minute?" Holly stopped the man at the entrance to the community room after the service. Now probably wasn't the best time to connect with him, but given her schedule, her choices were limited. And if she gave herself more time, she'd probably chicken out.

His gaze softened as he reached out, placed his hand on her shoulder and squeezed gently. "Of course. Did you want to talk here or in my office?"

She glanced back and forth across the crowded room. With the official kickoff of the holiday season now, energy filled the crowded space, yet seemed to miss her. She swallowed. Would she ever feel it again? Could she allow herself to? "Maybe outside in the foyer? I need to keep a look out for Cam."

"Of course. Right this way." He ushered her back into the foyer and over to a quiet corner. "What seems to be troubling you?"

Holly stared at the small pile of toys placed under the Christmas tree between the double doors leading into the sanctuary. Collecting presents for the less fortunate was a mission the church did every year. She and Jared used to donate, but that had stopped the year after he died. A lot of things did while she tried to deal and cope with her grief. She was still trying. But it was important to share what little she had with others who were less fortunate. And so was keeping a routine. And helping others.

"I—I'm— I don't know. I feel so lost and alone."

Pastor Matt rubbed his chin. "And this time of year doesn't help, does it?"

Holly shook her head.

"Survivor's guilt is a hard cross to bear. But you don't need to bear it. Jesus did it for us. He died so we might live. I know it's easier said than done, but search your heart. Challenge those irrational thoughts. You are not to blame, Holly. Grieve for Jared, but do not accept that responsibility. You did everything possible that night to keep yourselves safe."

"But I don't feel that I did. I took my eyes off the road. We were having an argument. I should have been paying better attention." The numbness that she associated with her thoughts of the accident surfaced again. Her fingernails dug into her palms and she bit down on her bottom lip.

"Who hasn't taken their eyes off the road at least once? Do you change your radio station? Or talk on your cell phone? Or look over at Cameron when you're talking?"

Holly nodded.

"Of course you do. I don't know of one person who can say that they pay attention one hundred percent of the time. Don't focus on the burden of guilt, Holly. God gave you a gift. You survived for Cameron. Each day He gives us is a gift. Use it wisely."

Holly closed her eyes for a moment and let his words sink in. Was there anything else she could have done that night? No. She hadn't been driving too fast, and she'd turned her steering wheel in the direction of the skid. But being on a hill with a sharp curve at the bottom along with the stand of trees…deep down, Holly knew that there was nothing she could have done.

Pastor Matt picked up her hand again and held it between his. "There are a few support groups in Flagstaff that gather weekly for people to help each other through their grief." Something caught his attention and he glanced over her shoulder, a pensive look coming into his eyes. "You're not the only one who needs to go."

Holly turned and met Ethan's gaze.

"Thanks, Pastor Matt."

He squeezed her hand gently before he released it. "Anytime, Holly. My door is always open."

Holly slipped back into the community room and found her son and Ethan, each with a plateful of food. "Mom, what are we doing later?"

Her son straightened his shoulders and lifted his chin. The top of his head almost reached her eye level. When had Cam sprouted up? And when had he lost his little-boy softness? And outgrown his clothes? His long sleeves barely came down to his wrists and his pants neared the flood stage. She had to siphon money from the grocery budget and take him shopping this week.

Holly knew Cameron wanted to go out to the sanctuary, and she thought about her schedule. She needed to talk to Ethan, though, before she made any commitments, in case he had other plans. "You have a rehearsal this afternoon."

"Do I have to do it?" Cam kicked the floor with his sneaker, a scowl on his face.

"Yes. Some things are not negotiable. The Christmas pageant was short of shepherds this year, and Mrs. Stocker needed more boys."

"They still do the Dynamite Creek Christmas pageant?"

"Yes. Next weekend at the old Jensen place outside of town. Not too far from the sanctuary, if I remember correctly. Pastor Matt does a wonderful job with the narration, but this year it could be interesting if it keeps snowing. Cam played baby Jesus when he was an infant." Holly's memories flew back to that night and the reaction of the crowd when they realized it was a real baby instead of a doll. Her heart swelled and a smile curved her lips. "Of course, he doesn't remember. Not that I'd expect him to, but it was still special just the same."

"I don't want to do it." Cam continued to scowl and kick the floor.

"Why not? It's an honor to be asked. Even I did it as a kid. Call it a rite of passage for the kids of Dynamite Creek." Ethan crossed his arms and raised an eyebrow, as if daring Cameron to challenge him.

"Really?" Cam's attitude spun a one-eighty.

"Really. I played a shepherd, too. I got to chase around Mr. McDermott's pesky goat all night and try to keep him from eating all the props. Do they still use live animals?"

"Yes, but not as many as they did years ago. The year before Cam's birth, the three wise men came in on camels, but now they use horses. And I think there might be a goat or a few sheep."

Cameron looked at Ethan with the hero worship Holly had uncomfortably grown accustomed to before her son high-fived him. "Fine. I'll do it, but only because you did. There's Tyson. I'll be right back."

While Cameron ran off to talk to his friend, Holly used the opportunity to speak her thoughts. She'd had all night to think about it, and this morning's sermon on opening your heart to receive all that God had to offer could have been written for her. She truly was blessed to have what she did even though there were days when it was easy to forget. Pastor Matt's stories of those who had lost everything in last month's hurricane moved her deeply and made her more aware that even when things looked the darkest, there was always a light to show you the way. You just had to be open to it.

And her talk with Pastor Matt a few minutes ago gave her more clarity on her role in the accident. She started to accept the idea that she wasn't really responsible at all.

"Look. I've been thinking about the wood shop. I—I— It's okay for you and Cameron to use it. I'm sorry I got so upset yesterday. It was just such a surprise to find you in there."

Cam was the one she really needed to tell, but

her son had withdrawn again, making it difficult for her to speak to him in the small amount of time they could actually spend together.

"I'm sorry we didn't ask permission." Ethan's gaze darted around the crowded room before he reached over and pulled her out of the way of a group of rambunctious teenagers.

His fingers remained on her arm, creating a crazy sensation again that she was afraid to put an emotion to. The unspoken kiss lingered in the air between them, yet Holly wasn't ready to bring it up. She swallowed the lump in her throat, stepped from his grasp and then wiped her hands against her black slacks.

"Apology accepted." Holly hated to have to say her next words but what choice did she have, especially when Kristen wasn't available? Sure, Cameron was old enough to be left alone for a few hours, but recent history, excluding the time he spent with Ethan, told her another story. She stared at the checkered pattern on the beige carpet before she met his gaze again. Money was finally coming in, but at what cost? She had less time than before, when she actually needed more time to spend with Cameron, but what bothered her more was her son didn't seem to care. After Christmas things would change. "I have to run and do a bid for a potential decorating job in an hour and then stop by to check on Mindy at the store before we leave for the rehearsal. If you don't mind taking Cam with you, you can use the shed. That way he can finish up whatever he was working on."

Later that afternoon, Ethan watched Cameron nail the last board into place. Fixing Holly's porch after they'd finished up in the woodworking shop reminded him of all the things that still needed to be done at the sanctuary and his house, for that matter. But teaching Holly's son the basics in carpentry and other useful skills could only be beneficial in the long run when he wouldn't be around. Not that Ethan had any plans of leaving Dynamite Creek, but everything eventually came to an end. As much as he'd love to keep Cameron around to help with the sanctuary and see that he followed the right path into adulthood, in another year or two, Cameron's thoughts would be elsewhere and Ethan would need the spot open to help another at-risk kid.

Using the back of his hand, he wiped the sweat from his forehead despite the cold, late-fall air around them. Stepping out the back door with a tray wedged against her hip, Holly looked so young in her faded Northern Arizona University sweatshirt. Too young to be a widow. But then again so was Stephanie Dodd, a young mother and the wife of one of the men killed under his watch. A senseless death. A needless one. If only he'd been doing his job right. Instead of looking for the ambush, he'd been distracted by the stray dog running around on the road. He'd been worried that the convoy would hit it.

No one should have died. He should have realized the dog had been a decoy. A movie reel of images tumbled around in his mind, the signals from his brain tossing around the contents of his stomach. He'd held Mike Dodd in his arms, his own blood mingling with Mike's as he tried to staunch the flow from his wounds. *I don't want to die. Say a prayer for me. Tell Steph that I love her, little Jacob, too.* His breaths came in gasps as he tried to talk while his life spilled out of him in a stream of red. Blood, dust and chemical smells surrounded them as did the sounds of moans and yelling and gunfire. Light had faded to black and the next thing Ethan knew, he was in a hospital in Germany.

"Are you okay?" Holly handed both Ethan and Cameron a glass of water.

"Fine." Ethan blinked and stared at the scenery around him, so different from the dusty brown of Afghanistan. He drank the entire contents in one try, but nothing could erase the memories that bombarded him now in the day-light hours, too.

Holly's eyebrows rose a fraction before she drew them in close, her breathing changing to a quicker tempo. "Thanks for fixing that for me, guys. Now I don't have to worry about anyone hurting themselves."

"Not a problem." Cameron straightened his shoulders again and looked at Ethan with trust and adulation written in his expression.

The boy misplaced his trust in him. Holly, too, because he was the wrong person. He'd be better off cutting any ties to them while he still had his heart intact. Or most of it, anyway. The kiss in the shed had affected him more than he cared to think about. He still needed to learn from his past mistakes before he could move forward.

And if she was looking for protection, she'd be better off with someone else.

At the store Thursday afternoon, Holly dug through the boxes she'd taken from Abby's place. The musty odor permeated the candy-cane-scented air and dust settled in her nose. She sneezed. Abby had been right. There wasn't much use for the stuff as it was, but she could turn some of it into other things. Maybe. If she could find the inspiration between all her worries.

"What do you think?" She held up some hand-painted wooden ornaments.

"Pretty ghastly. So is this." Kristen pulled out a bag of cheap plastic holly leaves and berries. "Although Figaro might like to play with it. So how's Ethan?"

Holly's heart fluttered at the mention of his name. She didn't dare tell Kristen about the kiss. Or her reaction to it. Her friend would only encourage the romance, if there was one, to continue. Confusion clouded her judgment. It had been so long since she'd been on the starting end of a relationship, she had no idea what the signs were anymore. "Okay, I guess."

"Only just okay? Don't you see each other every day?"

"Not always." At least not anymore, but she kept that information to herself. "Cam is usually waiting for me in the driveway when I pick him up."

He used to walk with Cameron to her car and say hi. What had changed over the past few days? She didn't have to rack her brain for too long. Heat seared her cheeks and her fingers instinctively found her mouth. The kiss must have affected him, too, and he realized as she did that any type of relationship between them was out of the question. Too bad her heart didn't seem to be following her head's lead.

"Regardless of what you think or want, there is nothing between us now, or will be in the future. I'm sure Ethan feels the same. Now, let's think of a way we can use all this stuff."

Holly wished she could wipe the knowing look flittering through Kristen's eyes. "I got it. No more talk about Ethan." She glanced down at the ornament in her hand. "It's interesting to think this stuff is older than we are."

"And hopefully we've aged better."

"Well, some of us have." Laughing, Kristen picked up a box of round, plastic ornaments of various colors.

"Look who's talking." Holly continued to pull things from the box. "I was hoping there would be something in here I could use."

"Yeah, someone was going for the cheesy, retro seventies look. You know, next year when Cam's looking for a costume, you can glue some old garland to a green sweatshirt and attach these and he can go as a vintage Christmas tree."

Holly sank back onto her heels and snapped her fingers. "That gives me an idea. My neighbor threw away some old picture frames and broken footstools. I can glue these onto them and create a unique montage to hang on the wall or place by the fireplace. Individually, these are awful, but put them together..." Holly laid a bunch of the ornaments on the floor and interspersed them with a few sprigs of the plastic holly leaves she'd torn from the stems. "And you've got something stunning."

"And instead of glass and a picture, you could put a mirror inside the frame or figure out how to make a candleholder out of it. Or use it as a door hanging instead of a traditional wreath. You could sell them in the shop to spruce up the remaining merchandise and put them up online. And why stop with Christmas?" Kristen's excitement filled the air.

"You're right. Old costume jewelry, buttons, broken antique dishes. Even old hardware." Holly fingered the silver ball she'd taken from the box before she held it up. Giddiness took hold, probably from lack of sleep. "Look. A tiny disco ball." She stood and pointed her finger in the air before jutting it down across the front of her body, and wiggled her hips. "I think I've just discovered another source of income."

Kristen joined her and jutted her hip out along with her arms. "And I bet you can pick up more real cheap at the thrift stores in Flagstaff as well as some vases. These cheap plastic balls would probably look pretty good wedged inside. And then you could glue some poinsettias or other holiday flowers around the bottom and even to the top."

"Or I can glue the ornaments and stuff to the vases and create one-of-a-kind centerpieces, too." Holly giggled and continued her little jig with the silver ornament dangling above her head.

"Mind if we join you?" Ethan stepped through the door after another man, carrying a notepad and tape measure.

Both Holly's and Kristen's laughter died. Holly shivered from the blast of cold air and dropped her hand with the ornament to her side, her moment of joy escaping like the warm air inside the shop. Ethan had brought another potential tenant inside.

Reality hit. What good would it do to make more stuff to sell when she would have no place to sell it?

A cold wind seeped through Holly's jacket as she sat on the blanket she'd brought to watch the pageant Saturday night at the old Jensen place. She was glad she'd told Cam to wear his long johns underneath his shepherd's outfit and wished she'd done the same. The cold from the ground had a way of penetrating the layers of cloth. She shivered, glad the production was only thirty minutes long. Her fingers curled around what remained of the cup of hot chocolate provided by Kiwanis Club.

Around her, the gathering crowd settled into their lawn chairs or blankets in the dim glow cast by the temporary lighting brought in for the event. To her right, the choir paged through their music; the only other words that would be spoken tonight would be Pastor Matt's. His voice broke the quiet murmur of the crowd, announcing the show would start in five minutes.

She glanced around, only too familiar with the setting. A stable had been set up directly in front of her, its thatched roof of palm fronds stirring in the light breeze. Two false, old, stucco housefronts faced her, creating the intimate feeling of a small town among the dead grass and dormant trees.

The old Jensen place was the perfect spot. Out in the country and away from the town's lights, she could get a real sense of what it was like to live before electricity. Sure, they had temporary lights set up so people wouldn't trip and fall, but the muted lights only cast the glow down. The inky black sky dotted with millions of stars and planets winked back at her in the frosty air.

"Mind if I join you?" Ethan held up another blanket and smiled down at her tentatively.

"You're here?"

"I wouldn't miss Cameron's acting debut for

anything. I even told him a few things about keeping the goats in line."

"Good things, I hope," Holly teased lightly.

Ethan feigned innocence and put his hand to his chest. "Of course."

That he would come and watch Cam's performance filled her with gladness. It would mean so much to her son. It meant a lot to her, even though she tried to deny that her heartbeat had accelerated and that she had someone to share the moment with. Glancing around, she realized there wasn't any other room near the front. She moved to the corner of her blanket, well aware that it would be a snug fit for both of them. Since there was no room for his blanket on the ground, Holly had a different use for it in mind as another small gust of wind rattled the remaining leaves on the trees surrounding the natural amphitheater. She patted the spot next to her. "Um, sure. Have a seat."

"In a second." After he dropped the blanket down and strode away, Holly pulled the wool over her lap before Ethan returned a few moments later with two cups pinched between his fingers. "I haven't had hot chocolate in years. Here's another one for you." He settled down next to her, still a little too close for her comfort.

"Thanks. I'm sure Cam will be glad you made it."

"How about you?" When he gazed into her eyes, all thought fled her mind and all the breath from her lungs. It had been a week since the kiss in the shed, yet only hours since she'd last thought of him. His name was constantly in Cam's vocabulary, his image not too buried in her memory, and his kiss still lingered on her lips.

"No comment. It got colder than I thought it would tonight." Her voice came out a whisper and she drank some hot chocolate to occupy herself. The warm liquid coated her tongue and warmed her from the inside as Ethan's gaze did from the outside.

Ethan shifted a bit closer to her as if trying to block out the slight breeze. "What time did you get here?"

"Five o'clock."

"Two hours ago? You didn't just drop Cameron off?"

"It seemed silly to drive home just to turn around and come back. I did get some reading done while I sat in my car until people started showing up."

"You're freezing. Here." He pulled the blanket from her lap, draped it over her shoulders and wrapped her up.

"Thanks." She snuggled into the blue wool, which felt like a warm embrace and smelled like him. For someone who wasn't interested in starting a new relationship, she sure had a funny perspective on things. Maybe? Her gaze swept across his maimed hand. He'd been injured and could have been killed during his tour of duty. It didn't matter, though, that his time of service was done now. She knew only too well how a life could change with a simple drive to a Chamber of Commerce function on a cold, snowy night.

A few moments of silence ensued, as if he was testing out a new topic before he spoke. "Looked like you were having fun the other day."

Embarrassment flushed her skin as she thought about her impromptu dance with Kristen. "I was a bit excited about some possibilities we discovered in that box of old Christmas stuff from the Bancroft Bed & Breakfast. If all goes well, I've just found another stream of revenue."

"So did I."

Those three simple words and his serious expression told her more than if he shouted it from the hill behind the makeshift stable.

"You found a new tenant for the store." She knew she should be happy for him, but she couldn't muster anything up. Breathing became a chore and her vision clouded.

"Yes. I'm sorry."

"You have nothing to be sorry for. That's business." Yet she couldn't keep the emotion from tainting her voice.

The electronic bong sounded, signaling the start of the pageant, but some of the sparkle was gone. All along she knew that she'd have to close the store, but knowing without a doubt it was a reality gripped her in a viselike hold. The death of a dream. Jared's dream. But having an end date also filled her with relief.

She could quit pretending, but she'd also have to put Jared's memory to rest, too.

Disloyalty stabbed at her and made her shiver again as the actors playing the townspeople took their places, some hanging laundry, a few tending to the fire, while others gathered around in conversation.

"You forgot gloves, didn't you?" Ethan whispered in her ear.

"It was enough just getting here on time. Cam wasn't exactly excited about coming."

"Yeah, well, to be honest, I wasn't too happy about doing it myself. It kind of ruins the reputation in school."

"Thanks for not sharing *that* part with Cam."

"You're welcome. Like I told him, it's a rite of passage." He picked up her free hand and held it between his as if trying to warm it but he never let go. It felt wrong and right to be sitting there holding his hand. Wrong because it might give people and Cameron the wrong impression if someone saw them, but just this moment right, because she felt as if she had someone she could lean on, depend on and help her through each day.

Mary, riding a donkey led by Joseph, strolled onto the scene. "Mary's my second cousin Deena's daughter, Lilly," Ethan said.

"So you had another reason for coming tonight. Why aren't you sitting with your family?" Holly whispered harshly so as not to disturb the performance for those around her. She knew he'd had to have had more family here than just his mother.

"Because there are too many of them and I prefer the view from over here much better." The warmth of his breath in her ear created havoc with her insides. Her friend was right. Ethan did like her. The kiss confirmed it, too. For both of them. It would only take a small movement of her head to connect with his lips and allow herself to feel again and bask under the attention.

No! Her back straightened and she focused on the scene playing out in front of her. Mary and Joseph had been turned away at the inn and the owner was showing them the stable.

The spotlight dimmed, and a soft tenor voice

filled the air. Holly allowed the music to swirl around her. She needed to focus on the play and not the man beside her.

"Look. There's Cam. The one in the blue with the off-white headpiece." Holly motioned her head toward the three boys walking up the trail with a sheep and two goats. After arriving at the predetermined spot, her son stretched his fingers toward the fire one of the older boys had started in the fire pit. Beside him a goat that kept trying to eat the rope was tied to his arm.

The audience twittered at the antics of Cameron trying to keep the goat from eating his costume while the chorus continued with another a capella carol.

Suddenly, from behind the hill, a spotlight beamed upon a teenage girl. In the darkness, she looked as if she were floating in the air, but Holly knew that she simply stood on a small platform on top. Still, the effect transported her back in time and filled her with wonderment, peace and hope.

"Do not be afraid. Behold, I bring tidings of great joy." Pastor Matt's voice floated out over the loudspeakers.

The words held double meaning for Holly.

A few heartbeats later, Mary revealed this year's baby Jesus. A wail ensued and the audience sighed.

"That part always gets to me." Holly gripped Ethan's hand tighter and leaned into him, absorbing his warmth and the feeling of protection. Moisture coated her eyes.

Maybe because it represented God's love for them that he gave His only son. Or maybe that it represented a new beginning.

Chapter Ten

"Where are we going?" Cameron's voice filled the interior of Ethan's SUV.

The boy apparently didn't like to get up early on the weekends, especially after his performance last night and the ice cream that followed. Ethan smiled to himself. The day had dawned bright and sunny, but that was expected to change later in the afternoon when another storm moved through right on the heels of the four inches they received last night. Now that the church service was over, it was the perfect day to chop down a Christmas tree. Or two. Or four.

"You'll see." He smiled at Holly, who returned it readily. Something had changed between them yesterday, and he liked it. She seemed a bit more relaxed, more settled, even though he'd admitted he'd found a new tenant for the shop. Guilt consumed him. He had no choice, though. He needed the rent money to help him pay his own bills while the sanctuary got off the ground.

"Cam's not a morning person."

"I've already figured that out. He'll grow out of it. Eventually." Just like the boy would grow out of his troubles. He was at a tough age. For now, Ethan was glad he was there to help guide him in the right direction.

"Are we going to the sanctuary?" Cameron's excited voice popped up from the backseat. "Are you almost done, Mr. P.? When are you going to move the dogs?"

"Yes, we are. We made a lot of headway this past week. If all goes well, we'll be in by Christmas."

"But how will I be able to get out here after school?"

Ethan didn't have an answer. "We'll worry about that when the time comes."

The snow hit Holly on the back of her head. She turned just in time to see another snowball flying through the air. "Hey!"

Both her son and Ethan had reloaded behind the quick barrier they'd built in the dog run. She ducked behind a pine tree and scooped up a handful of fresh snow. Heavy and moist, the snow was perfect for packing. Forming it into a perfect ball, she waited for one of the two to expose themselves. She didn't have to wait long. She hurled the ball and it hit Ethan square in the chest.

"Good shot."

"My mom was captain of the softball team. She was an all-star pitcher. I'm switching sides." Cam lunged from behind the snowbank and headed toward her. But not before Holly lobbed another perfect pitch and hit her son in the chest.

"Mom."

"Hey, all's fair in love and war." Yet she gave him the opportunity to hide behind the pine tree with her and lob a few more snowballs at Ethan until he cried uncle.

"Wow, I can't believe you really got beaten by a girl." His laughter filled the air as Cam ran from behind the tree, plopped onto his back into the fresh snow and began to move his arms and legs. A smile creased her lips. Holly hadn't seen her son this happy in a long time, and she owed it all to Ethan.

"Yeah, well, until you switched sides, you were, too." Holly helped Ethan dust the snow from his sleeve, but his amused expression told her he didn't mind. It hadn't really been a fair fight, but Ethan didn't seem to care.

"You are a good shot." The corners of his

eyes crinkled as he squinted from the glare of the sun. "Is there anything else I should know about you?"

"I can't sing, I love sushi and I placed fifth in the state spelling bee in eighth grade." Feeling a bit childish herself, Holly let her reserve down and jumped in the snow next to her son. Cold bit her neck as she moved her arms and legs in a wide sweeping motion.

"A brainy athlete. That's an oxymoron if I ever heard one."

"Hey, I resent that." She grabbed a handful of snow and threw it up at him.

"What word did you place with?"

"Metamorphosis. M-e-t-a-m-o-r-p-h-o-s-i-s. Metamorphosis." She grinned. "Okay, smarty-pants, do you know what that even means?"

Ethan sank down beside her. "Of course. It's a transformation of one thing into another. Like a caterpillar into a butterfly."

A strange feeling passed through her. It was as if after two years, she was starting to break free of her shell and stretch her wings. In the Bible, it was the symbol for the Resurrection. Was she going through her own sort of change? She shook off the feeling. "But can *you* spell it?"

"I'm not even going to try. What word did you miss?"

"*Parliament.* I forgot the second *a*. But enough about that. Let's build a snowman. You make the base. I'll make the middle, and you make the head, Cam." Holly jumped to her feet. With the wet, heavy snow, they should be able to build a monstrous one that would take days or weeks to melt if the cold snap held up.

"You're on." Ethan pushed himself from the snow and formed another snowball. He gazed at her playfully and tossed it in the air.

"Don't even think about it," Holly warned as she molded her own ball. "I went easy on you last time."

Ethan laughed and started rolling the snowball around to form a bigger one.

Once assembled, the three balls of snow needed to be adorned. Holly took her hat from her head and placed it on top. Cam trudged to the edge where the woods met the snowdrift and broke off a few dead branches from a tree.

"Too bad we don't have a carrot." Ethan pulled out a few pennies from his pocket and placed them in as eyes and a nose. Then he removed his scarf and wrapped it around the snowman's neck.

"Now all we need is a mouth. If I had my purse, I probably could have found something in there to use." Holly shrugged. "But it seemed ridiculous to bring it out here."

"Why would you? We're going to have our hands full with the next activity. Cameron, there should be some rocks around here somewhere. Check the areas where the snowballs lifted the snow. If you can't find anything, then there should be some pinecones by the pine tree near where you got the arms."

"I'm on it." Cameron dashed away, a jumble of arms and legs. The corners of her mouth turned up. When he grew into his adult body, he'd tower over her, thanks to the Stanwyck side of his DNA.

After scooping up some snow, Ethan filled in an uneven spot on the snowman's trunk. "He's a good kid. He'll be okay."

"I know he will. Thanks for all your help." Holly readjusted the scarf around the snowman's neck. "Aren't you cold?"

"Aren't you? Heat escapes from your head."

"It does, but I'm used to this weather. You're not." Her fingers played with the scarf's dark fringe. Even though she couldn't feel the fabric through her gloves, she could imagine the rough wool texture against her skin. And if she dared think hard enough, she could almost feel Ethan's five-o'clock shadow against her palms, his lips caressing hers again. This time she wasn't sure if she would break it off so quickly.

Disloyalty stabbed at her heart.

"I'll be fine, but if it makes you feel better, we can come retrieve our stuff on the way back to the house." Ethan must have sensed her discomfort. "Are you okay?"

"I'm fine. Thanks for bringing us out here. We haven't had this much fun since—" Holly stopped short. The memories of Jared and their last winter together as a family surfaced. They'd gone sledding, had their own snowball fights and built a snowman, just days before the accident.

And in the blink of an eye—or tires against black ice—everything had changed.

Ethan gathered her in his arms and rocked her gently. The light kiss on the top of her head brought back more thoughts about her late husband. Letting go was hard when everything around her reminded her of what she'd lost.

But Kristen was right. She had to. Today brought that to the forefront. Somehow, somewhere feelings had surfaced for Ethan regardless of her attempts to close off her heart. The realization stung. She had to let go and move on. Living in the past wasn't healthy, but as Pastor Matt pointed out, she wasn't the only one who needed to realize that.

Shrugging out of his arms, Holly stepped away into some sort of hole buried by the snow. Her arms flailed as she tried to regain her equilibrium and footing. Not happening. She fell backward onto her bottom, the snow quickly finding its way under her jacket and sweater. She shivered, but it was more from Ethan's unguarded expression than from the cold.

"Are you okay?" He held out his hand.

"Just fine." But she knew her heart would never be the same.

Ethan released Holly's hand when he heard Cameron approach. Her son might misconstrue the gesture, especially after their conversation on Thanksgiving. Cameron wanted another dad and someone to make his mom happy, make her laugh again.

Ethan wasn't the guy to do that. People had counted on him before, depended on him for their lives, and he'd let them and their families down. But holding Holly in comfort had been the most natural thing in the world. Ethan took another step to the side, stooped down and packed on more snow to another uneven spot on the base of the snowman.

She glanced at him from underneath her lashes as if she understood, before her attention turned to her son. "What did you find, Cam?"

He held out his hands. "Pinecones. They were bigger than the rocks."

"Pinecones it is, then." Ethan stood and

dusted the snow from his gloves. "Since you retrieved them, you may have the honors."

Once the snowman was complete, Ethan grabbed the saw he'd dropped by the edge of the meadow before the snowball fight. "Come on, our ultimate destination is just a bit farther."

They walked in a companionable silence through the woods. Ethan loved the stillness of the day, the crisp air filling his lungs, the muffled footsteps on the fresh snow. An occasional bird cawed, and a few rabbits scattered when they wandered too close. Not wanting to disturb the peace surrounding them, he put a finger to his lips. "If we're real quiet, we may see a deer or two."

"Really? That would be cool," Cameron whispered back.

Too bad the deer chose not to cooperate. A few minutes later, they stepped into what should have been another meadow, but this one was filled with pine trees of various sizes.

Holly gasped beside him. "Wow. It's beautiful."

"Cool." Cameron ran into the stand of trees.

"Cam—"

"Let him go. He'll be okay." Holly's wide-eyed wonder and look of pure enjoyment of his special retreat pleased him. He knew the feeling. He'd been nine when his dad first brought him out here—a family ritual that took place at that special age. Eyes wide, mouth open, he'd run through the trees, arms outstretched, touching the spiny needles, laughing. They'd played hide-and-seek before deciding the right ones to cut down. His smile turned upside down.

It was also their last Christmas together. His dad had been dead for almost twenty-five years now, and Ethan still missed him. Bringing company out here with him might have been a mistake. He identified with Holly's son and knew what Cameron faced in the future.

While there was nothing Ethan could do to bring Jared back, he could make things better for Cameron, just like his old neighbor did for him. He glanced up. *Thank you, Lord, for bringing me into Cameron's life right now and helping him through this.*

Other images superimposed themselves in his mind's eye. He clenched his fists, realizing there was nothing he could do to bring those people back, either.

But he wasn't responsible for his father's death.

"Are you okay?" Holly placed a hand on his arm and knitted her eyebrows. His muscles bunched underneath her touch. "You have that faraway look in your eyes."

"Fine." He blinked. "I was just thinking about my first time here."

"Really? Then it's not a pleasant one. You're tense. If it's that painful, we can leave, but I have a feeling this has nothing to do with here but someplace far away. Afghanistan is behind you now." She knew him well, but not well enough.

"You don't understand. It will never be behind me."

"Only if you want it to be that way." Her voice softened and her gloved fingers ran up and down his arm. "You weren't the one who planted the bomb." He knew she was trying to help, but her words had the opposite effect.

"No, but I should have seen the signs. I should have recognized that they knew my weakness for dogs." Anger boiled inside him, begging for release. He should have brought an ax, but he doubted that the four trees he needed to cut down would be enough to release him from the tension.

"You weren't the only one there. There were others who could have recognized them, too. What about the driver?" Her words struck a blow.

"But it was my job."

"And given the circumstances, I'm sure you did your best. Things happen. Just like the night Jared died." Holly's face resembled the snow around them. "I know what you're going through."

His anger dissipated into the air as he gathered her in his arms and held her close, inhaling her floral fragrance. He needed to gain control over his emotions and deal with what happened. Everyone told him it would take time. That the nightmares would cease; that he would recover emotionally as he did physically. Maybe Holly could help him. Or maybe this was something he had to do on his own.

But until he did, there could be nothing between him and Holly, despite his growing love for her. It wouldn't be fair to her or her son. He broke away moments before Cameron rejoined them.

"Look what I found." Giving them a strange look, Cameron held out his hands. Five small pinecones dotted his gray gloves. "I want to exchange these for the ones I put on the snowman. These are better." He handed them to Holly. "Here. Please hold them. This place is so cool. Why are the trees all in rows?"

"A long time ago, my great-grandfather decided to plant some pines right after he built the house and barn so we'd always have a supply of fresh Christmas trees. Once spring hits,

I'll be planting a few more to replace the ones we take today."

"Can I help? How many are we going to chop down?"

"Well, let's see. I need one, so does my cousin Meredith, and my mom needs one. Am I missing anyone?"

"We need a tree, right, Mom?" Cam rubbed his hands together and tilted his head forward. His eyes widened in expectation.

Holly thought about the fake tree in the garage. They were easier to handle, but nothing compared to the real thing, especially the smell. Candle companies only wished they could bottle the scent.

"I believe we do. Which one do you think would be the perfect one?"

"Let me look."

As they tramped through the trees, searching for the perfect ones, birds chirped, and the sound of snow underfoot met her ears. Holly inhaled the earthy scent, unique to the area after a snowfall, mingled with that of pine.

Her mood lightened a bit, but some of the thrill had disappeared. Their guilt was the white elephant in the room that no one wanted to talk about. They both wore it like jackets that couldn't be shed.

Mindless of the slight tension between the adults, Cameron led them to an eight-foot-tall pine. "This one right over here."

"Are you sure? It might be too tall." Ethan looked at her. "What height is your ceiling?"

"Ten feet."

"This one it is, then."

Holly's heart filled with misgivings and joy at the sight of the two heads bowed together as Ethan showed Cameron how to hold the saw and cut the tree at the base. Cameron had blossomed over the weeks that Ethan had been working with him. He was turning back into the boy she remembered. But it should have been his father out here with him, and Holly had taken that away from him.

She let out a slow breath and digested Pastor Matt's words.

She couldn't control the weather that night or the patch of ice, and she'd done everything possible to avoid the collision. There was nothing more she could have done. A few snowflakes drifted by her visions as she glanced up past the dark, gray, snow-laden clouds, searching for an answer. Searching for God.

"There. It's up." Ethan dusted his hands against his jeans and stepped back. "Good job,

Cameron. You've just put up your first live Christmas tree."

"Sweet." Her son beamed with pride. "Look, Mom."

"Awesome job. This calls for some hot chocolate." Holly carried the tray with three cups into the living room, the scent of chocolate mingling with the pine. Her heart rate changed when her fingers touched Ethan's as he accepted his cup. She tried to shake off the sensation that reminded her of the kiss in the shed. She'd been in a vulnerable position then and still was, with her emotions so close to the surface in recent weeks, and they were all due to the man fluffing up the branches of the pine tree.

"Thanks." Cameron grabbed his cup and settled down on the area rug covering the hardwood floor. Sighing, he leaned back on the plush sofa and crossed his legs in front of him before he took a sip. "Okay, the hard part's done. Don't we have to check on the dogs, Mr. P.?"

"Oh, no you don't. Don't get too comfortable. Now the real fun begins." Holly snapped her fingers and pointed at her son. "You don't get off that easily. Decorating is part of the deal. It's my favorite part. It's yours, too, remember?" Good thing, too, because she was doing a lot of that lately. Not that she didn't appreciate the extra money coming in; she did. Her gaze rose to the ceiling, and she managed to send up a silent prayer of thanks. Things were starting to get better. She had another job tomorrow for Mrs. Baker, another member of the congregation, to put up her tabletop tree and a few other decorations.

"Mooom."

"Don't Mom me. You know Figaro's only good for swatting the ornaments off the bottom of the tree. The lights go first, then the garland, then the ornaments and finally the star. Got it?"

"Got it." Her son sulked but pushed himself off the floor.

Holly wanted to wipe the amused grin from Ethan's face. "You're not off the hook, either, mister. Everyone under this roof is expected to help."

Ethan held up his hands in mock surrender. "Looks like we're stuck, Cameron. The boss has spoken."

"And don't forget it." Holly laughed, took a sip of her hot chocolate and sat back on her heels. The laughter felt good. The foreign sound had appeared at the most unlikely times in the past few weeks, and she owed it to one man.

Ethan caught her son's attention. "Your job for the next few weeks, besides the sanctuary, is going to be making sure there's water in the base every day. A dry Christmas tree could cause a fire."

"Got it."

Holly dug into the box marked Lights and pulled out a strand of multicolored ones. Before she could stand, Cameron walked over and held out his hand. "Here, let me have those. Let's put up the lights, Mr. P."

Reluctantly, Holly handed them over. Despite her earlier words about Ethan helping, somehow when she envisioned putting up the decorations a few weeks ago, it was her and Cameron doing the work together. The idea that she'd been pushed aside hurt, yet Cam's smile and willingness to help couldn't be overlooked.

"Come on, Holly. You're not going to let the men do all the work, now, are you?" Ethan held out his hand and pulled her to her feet.

"Of course not." But maybe she should, since her reaction to him seemed to grow stronger with each passing heartbeat.

"You're the decorator. Where should the lights go?"

"On the tree, of course, although the rest of these are all tangled. I have an idea. Cam, we need some help here."

"What?" Her son joined them at the box.

"We need to get these organized so it's easier

to get them on the tree. Here." She handed a ball of tangled lights to her son. "Now, Ethan, you just stay right there and hold this." She found the plug and handed it to him, a smile on her lips. "Okay, now, as we unravel the lights, Ethan is going to be our human holder. Ethan, all you have to do is turn slowly so we can wrap them around you."

Cameron's laughter joined hers. "Cool idea, Mom."

A few minutes later, the first strand had been untangled and wrapped around Ethan's middle.

"I have another idea." Excitement and humor filled Cam's voice as he plugged in the extension cord and ran back to Ethan. "I'm gonna light you up."

The lights cast a multicolored glow on Ethan. Holly ran back to another box labeled Decorations and pulled out a hat. She flipped on the switch and placed the singing Christmas tree on his head. The tree wiggled around as the music filled the air while she and Cameron lifted their arms up and began to dance around Ethan, singing along with the song. Holly's laughter filled the air again. When had she lost the ability to have fun? The thought sobered her when she realized that only one person was responsible for how she felt.

And she suddenly found herself alone with

him when Cam left the room to run upstairs to get his camera.

Holly stopped dancing and stood in front of Ethan, close enough to take in the clean scent of the outdoors underneath the fragrance of the tree. His eyes clouded with an emotion she hadn't seen for a while and her breath stalled.

Ethan placed his hand under her chin, forcing her to stare into his compassionate eyes. The scent of peppermint collided with the freshness of pine and pulled her to him. Holly wrapped her arms around his neck, needing to feel his warmth, his protectiveness, his trust. She claimed his lips. It was meant to be a light kiss, the kind between friends, but deepened into something more. Ethan made her feel alive again, and if she had to admit it, she enjoyed the kiss way more than the first time. Holly couldn't deny it any longer. She'd fallen completely in love with him.

Hearing Cameron tread on the stairs, she blinked to end the connection. Before taking a step backward, she removed the hat and tossed it toward the coffee table.

"Walk over to the tree, and as soon as Cam takes your picture, we'll transfer the lights."

Once all the lights were on and the garland in place, Holly pulled out a pewter Noah's Ark scene and motioned for her son. "Cam, here's your first ornament. And here's the ornament you made in Mrs. Beasley's kindergarten class." Holly held up the round wreath made out of construction paper with uncooked macaroni pasta glued to the outside and Cam's picture inside the circle.

Cameron blushed. "Mom."

"What? It's cute. Maybe we should make more ornaments this year."

"No way!" Her son retreated behind the tree with a bunch of ornaments in his hand. "Hey, aren't you going to help, Mr. P.?"

Ethan settled back in the armchair and put his hands behind his head. "No. I helped with the hard stuff and need a break. This is between you and your mom. Besides, I've got my own tree to decorate, and you can help with that tomorrow after your homework and chores."

The tree filled up quickly with ornaments.

"And now for the finishing touch." Holly handed her son the tree topper.

Cameron scampered up the old, rickety wood ladder to place the star on the top.

The rung broke beneath his left foot. Cameron tried to regain his balance, his arms flailing out, grasping for something to latch on to. He swayed, tilted and fell backward.

Cries escaped both Holly's and Cameron's lips. Bile hit the back of Ethan's throat and adrenaline burned in his veins. But just like before, he was powerless to stop the chain reaction of events. He stood and moved forward, but it wasn't quick enough. As if in slow motion, Ethan watched Cameron hit the floor with a thud and lie next to the ladder.

Please, Lord, don't let him be hurt.

"Cameron! Sweetie, are you okay?" Holly dropped to her knees, her eyes wide and all the blood drained from her face when she saw the unnatural bulge near his wrist. With a shaky hand, she pushed the hair from his face. "Everything's going to be okay."

Her gaze met his, looking for confirmation. Ethan knelt down, tasting the fear. "Don't move, Cameron. Let me see what we're dealing with."

The boy nodded, pain creasing the skin around his eyes. His gaze scanned the floor and Cameron's arm. No blood or exposed bone, just a bump where the bone had snapped from the pressure. At least he was dealing with a simple fracture. "You've broken your arm. Does anything else hurt?"

This time Cameron shook his head.

Ethan's fingers probed up and down Cameron's other arm and legs. "Can you wiggle your fingers and toes?"

The boy did as instructed. Good. Nothing

else appeared to be broken, but he needed immediate medical attention.

"That's great, but don't move again." Ethan took control of the situation. "Holly, after you get a bag of ice, I'll go get my first-aid kit from the SUV. I have something to make a sling, which will hold his arm in place until we can get him to the E.R."

Snow accumulating on the roads, along with encroaching darkness, made driving treacherous. In the backseat, Holly gripped the strap of her seat belt with one hand and held on tightly to Cam as Ethan's headlights barely made a dent in the whiteness swirling around them. Holly kept talking to a minimum, wanting Ethan to give his full attention to driving. Still, she could tell Ethan fought to maintain control, given the whiteness of the knuckles on his left hand as he gripped the steering wheel.

Another incident rose to the forefront, except it was Holly driving and fighting the conditions because Jared had had a headache. Her hands clenched as the memories paralyzed her. She fought to push them back where they belonged. That time was over and done. This was here and now. Everything would be okay. It had to be.

"Stop it, Mom. You're hurting me even more," Cam whispered from the middle seat.

"Sorry." Holly quit squeezing so hard and worried her bottom lip as the snow consumed everything around them.

Ethan's wheels lost traction on the pavement when he attempted to stop at a stop sign. Nausea roiled in her stomach as the SUV fishtailed but managed to stop just shy of the intersection.

At this rate, it would take them at least fifteen minutes to get to the hospital, but going any faster would be unsafe. *Please, Lord, keep us safe. Let us get to the hospital in one piece.* Repeating the prayer over and over, she clutched the gold cross she'd pulled from her jewelry box.

It felt good to be right with the Lord.

"Hang on!"

Holly felt the wheels spin as Ethan tried to gain traction and move through the intersection. Her gaze froze on the red car speeding toward them from the driver's side. Ethan tried to move the SUV forward, but he wasn't fast enough and the other car blew the stop sign and clipped the back of his vehicle.

Holly wrapped her arms around Cam's shoulders, squeezed her eyes shut and held on tightly as the SUV spun on the ice and snow. Time suspended as she waited for the vehicle to stop, the thud of metal against metal still reverberating in her ears. She grew dizzy and her stomach dropped to the floor as she braced for impact.

Another thud jolted them inside the vehicle, and then muffled silence. Beside her, Cam whimpered in pain.

Holly lifted her head, opened her eyes and found Cam staring back at her. She gave him a quick once-over. He was okay. She kissed the top of his head and then looked beyond him. Glass fragments littered the empty seat behind Ethan's and cold wind and snow blew in through the shattered windows. They'd jumped the curb and were wedged up against a brick building, the driver's side caved in from the impact. Her heart stalled when she spied Ethan slumped over the steering wheel.

"Ethan!" There was no movement in the front seat.

No! Not again. *Please, Lord. Not again.*

"Stay where you are, Cam." It took two attempts for Holly to free herself from her seat belt so she could scramble out the undamaged door. The cold wind bit at her nose and exposed skin as she opened the door and forced her way into the front passenger seat.

"Is he okay, Mom?"

"I don't know, Cam. I don't know." *Please, Lord, let him be okay.* Holly managed to wedge her hands between Ethan and the steering wheel and maneuver him back so he leaned against the seat. She cradled Ethan's head between her hands. Blood poured from the open cut on his scalp, but he didn't regain consciousness. "Ethan. Please. Wake up."

Tears burned her eyes. She loved him. There was definitely no denying it now.

Her fingers shook violently as she reached back for her purse and dumped the contents onto the seat, searching for her phone to call for help.

Chapter Eleven

Sitting in the front seat of the ambulance, Holly dug her fingernails into her palms and chewed her bottom lip, the paramedic beside her concentrating on driving. She closed her eyes, unable to look at the bleak scenery. She shivered. The scene replaying in her head wasn't any better than staring at the blizzard outside. Over and over the images replayed in her mind and the jarring sensation of spinning out of control consumed her.

There was nothing she could have done. Nothing Ethan could have done.

"We're almost there, Mrs. Stanwyck."

Holly opened her eyes. Amid the swirl of white, Dynamite Creek Memorial stood out in red letters against the tan brick building as they turned into the parking lot. She swallowed and her breathing came in short, erratic bursts when they pulled up to the E.R. entrance. She hadn't been here since the first accident.

Moments later, she hurried across the pavement, her steps keeping tempo with her heartbeat as she followed behind the paramedics pushing the stretcher carrying Ethan and the man in dark green scrubs pushing Cameron in the wheelchair. The door snicked open and she stepped inside the foyer; the odor of antiseptic filled her nostrils. Another wave of nausea hit her.

A woman looked up from her clipboard. "Please take Cameron Stanwyck to Room 1 and Ethan Pellegrino to Room 7."

Hesitation racked her as Holly glanced between her son and a now-conscious Ethan. She needed to be there for both of them, but how could she be in two rooms at once? Ethan refused to meet her gaze, though, and her heart cried out as he was wheeled away in the opposite direction. He had shut her out.

Holly followed Cameron.

"Is he allergic to anything?" the nurse asked as she transferred Cam to the hospital bed.

"No. No allergies that I'm aware of." Still running on adrenaline and fear, Holly moved to Cam's side and pushed the hair off his forehead. She caught her lip between her teeth again. How small and fragile he looked, seemingly lost among the white sheets in the adult-size hospital bed. And scared.

"I'm going to give him some morphine for the pain. Is that okay?"

"Fine." Wanting to give the nurse some space, Holly sank down in the chair opposite the bed. Now that they were at the hospital, she acknowledged the pounding behind her eyelids and that her stomach had twisted into knots until she thought she was going to taste what remained of her lunch.

How was Ethan doing? Was his head wound serious? Did he suffer any other injuries? She clenched her hands and bit down hard enough to taste blood, staring at the heart-monitoring machine when the nurse inserted the IV for a morphine drip into Cameron's left arm.

"Hi." An older man in a white lab coat entered the room. "I'm Doctor Hill. Let's see what we have here." He went straight to the bed and examined Cam's arm. "Yep, I'd say it's broken. Now, how did you happen to do this?"

After listening to the story, he pulled a small flashlight from his pocket and looked into Cameron's eyes. "Good. No concussion. We're going to take a few X-rays, young man, and then I'm going to set it. Then you can get out of here when the snow lets up, but no roughhousing for a while."

A few moments later, another staff member came in. Holly held the hand on Cam's unbroken arm as they wheeled the bed into another room.

"Okay, Mom, you're going to need to stand behind that wall with the window while I'm taking the pictures." The woman in the dark blue scrubs motioned to her left.

"Cam, I need to go check on Ethan." Holly squeezed her son's hand. She didn't want to leave her son, yet she had to know how badly Ethan was hurt. "Will you be okay?"

Cam nodded.

"Are you sure?"

"Mom."

"I'll be right back, then." She kissed Cam on the forehead and then retreated from the room.

Holly's heart fluttered as she made short work of the distance between the rooms. There was nothing she could do for her son right now, and she needed to know that Ethan was going to be okay. He'd taken the brunt force of the crash and looked as if he'd lost a fair amount of blood. She glanced down at the dark red drops staining the sleeve of her jacket. Ethan's blood. Another sob wedged its way into her throat. He had to be okay. She couldn't lose him, too.

"Hi." Holly knocked as she peeked into Ethan's room. Aside from the large bandage covering the wound on his forehead and being slightly pale, he looked good. Better than good. He was alive. "How are you feeling?"

"Like I got hit by a brick building."

"Funny. Very funny. Glad to see you didn't lose your sense of humor." Holly wedged her hands onto her hips and strode to the bed. "You gave us quite a scare back there, mister."

"How's Cameron's arm?"

"They're taking X-rays right now and then the doctor is going to set it. What about you?"

He stared at a spot behind her shoulder. "So far just the cut, but they're going to keep me here for a few more hours to do more tests."

Holly's stomach flip-flopped again. Was there something going on that he wasn't telling her about? She searched his self-loathing expression. "Quit blaming yourself, Ethan. You kept us as safe as you could. The accident wasn't your fault. In fact, it could have been a lot worse. What if the other driver had T-boned us?"

"It doesn't matter. I failed in my duty." His gaze shifted back to hers, yet she knew he didn't see her but the horrific scene from all those months ago that replayed in his mind. Anguish and pain distorted the features that she'd come to love.

"No, you didn't." Holly refused to back down. "This isn't your fault." She reached out and touched him, ran her palms across his face.

The day's growth on his jawline was rough yet welcoming as she pressed her lips against his, trying to push away their nightmares.

He turned his head. "Allow me some dignity, Holly. This was all my fault. I can't keep anyone safe. Tell Cameron I can't have him out at the sanctuary anymore. You, either."

"Here, take this. How're you feeling?" Holly handed Cam the painkiller and a glass of water later that night. She sat down on the side of the bed and pushed away his bangs again.

"My arm hurts."

"Well, that's only to be expected. The painkiller from the hospital is starting to wear off, but what I just gave you should kick in soon."

"I'm sorry, Mom." Cam sat up in bed and hugged her as best he could with his good arm. Emotion laced his voice. "I was only trying to be helpful. If I hadn't fallen, I wouldn't have broken my arm and then we wouldn't have had to go to the hospital and Mr. P. would be okay."

"Of course you were trying to be helpful, sweetie." The endearment slipped out, but Cameron didn't seem to mind, even though he'd been embarrassed lately when she showed him any affection. She held him close and rested her cheek on the top of his head. "Ethan is going to be okay. He simply had a cut on his forehead and they were keeping him for a bit to make sure there was nothing else wrong."

"But if I hadn't broken my arm—"

"Shh. It was an accident. It could have happened anytime, anywhere. Accidents happen."

Accidents happen.

There was nothing Ethan could have done to prevent what happened today, just as she realized there was nothing she could have done two years earlier. Too bad Ethan didn't believe that. He was still consumed by a past that refused to release its grip.

No longer would she allow her past to continue to rule her life. She'd had a taste of happiness again and so had Cam. She was also sure that Ethan had felt it, too. Ethan. His image rose in her mind's eye. The caring and compassionate man had become a part of both her and Cam's lives. Maybe she could help him. If he'd let her. Which wasn't going to happen in the immediate future.

Giving her son one last gentle squeeze, she held him away from her and steadied herself for her next words. "But just like you, Ethan is having a hard time with what happened tonight. He doesn't want you out at the sanctuary anymore."

"Just until my permanent cast is on, right?"

How could she explain this when she didn't really understand the reasons herself? "No. You won't be going back at all. It's what he wants and we have to respect his wishes." She leaned down and kissed him on the forehead, hating to have to be the one to break the bad news to her son. "Good night."

Cam shrugged out of her grasp and hugged the covers to his chest, his expression laced with pain, disappointment and denial.

She left Cameron's room and lifted her gaze heavenward, staring at the ceiling before closing her eyes and breathing deeply. *I get it now, Lord. I understand. You give and You take away. Let go.* She had a lot of letting go to do. God knew what He was doing. By shutting the window, He was opening a door for her. She had to be ready to accept the new phase in her life by shedding the past and allowing a future into her heart. Pastor Matt was right. She had enough room in her heart to love a lot of people, Ethan included.

Her memories spun back to earlier that day when they cut down the Christmas trees, and she smiled.

Metamorphosis.

That was what she needed. In her life with Jared she'd been a caterpillar. When he'd died, she'd formed a cocoon and hid from the world. Now she was ready to break free from the chrysalis and start over as a new person.

Peace settled across her shoulders. She knew what she had to do. She didn't know what the future held for her, but she had to be ready to grasp it when it came.

"Cam?" Holly knocked on her son's door at six o'clock. He should be up by now. "Wake up. How are you feeling? You should be going to school in just over an hour."

No sound came from behind the door. Her stomach muscles clenched, upsetting the cup of coffee and yogurt she'd taken at breakfast.

"Cam? Come on, honey, it's time to wake up." She turned the handle, stepped across the threshold and flipped on the light switch.

Her son's bed was empty.

And not just empty; it looked as if Cam hadn't even tossed and turned in it last night. Sagging against the door frame, disbelief then terror ignited her blood. "Not funny, Cam. Where are you?"

As if her feet moved independently of her body, she entered the room and pulled back the sheets. Nothing. Not that she expected to see him without the telltale lump, yet her fingers ran up and down the cold fabric. She searched his closet, pushing his clothing aside, his old karate equipment, and even rummaged through the plastic bin of old cars. Then she checked every room in the house. Staggering back to his bedroom, she grasped the back of the chair to his desk and toppled it, daring to hope he'd wedged himself underneath.

Nothing.

"Cam? Please don't do this to me." She crawled back to the bed, tears ravaging her cheeks as she lifted the bed skirt and stared into the inky void. Not even Figaro hid in his favorite spot. In a vain attempt to find her son, she stretched out her arm and swept the area, only coming up with a few stray socks and one of his old Cub Scout T-shirts. She buried her face in the cotton. Cameron had run away.

Hoping that they'd released Ethan from the hospital last night, Holly grabbed her phone, her fingers stumbling across the buttons three times before she managed to dial his number. Cam had to be with him. He had to be, although she had no idea how he'd walk all the way across town in the dark. Clutching the phone like a lifeline, Holly clenched her other fist and pounded her knuckles against her forehead. "Answer the phone, Ethan. Please, answer the phone."

Her stomach clenched with each ring and her teeth worried her bottom lip. Maybe Ethan was outside with the dogs? Maybe he didn't realize that Cameron was supposed to be getting ready for school? Maybe they never released him and something far more serious was wrong with him? More panic twisted her emotions.

By the time his voice mail picked up, she'd already circled her kitchen twice. Holly hung up and reached for her winter jacket thrown across the kitchen chair. She had to do something.

Darkness pressed against the kitchen window. From outside, the sound of the wind chimes on her back porch echoed in her brain as she shoved her arms through the sleeves. Adrenaline spurred her out the door. Cold enveloped her in its icy grasp and her foot stumbled on the bottom step, but she continued to her car. After she rubbed her chilled, damp hands against her jacket, her fingers shook as she jammed the keys into the ignition.

Fifteen minutes later, Ethan answered the door as soon as she knocked. He looked good— really good— despite the accident last night. A bandage covered the cut on his forehead, but other than that, he showed no other signs of trauma. "Holly? Is everything okay? I tried to call you back but there was no answer. You didn't answer your cell phone, either."

Instead of soothing her, it set off another chain reaction of emotions. Holly bit back another sob. She must have left her cell phone on her nightstand. What if Cam was trying to call her? More fear gripped her lungs, making it impossible to breathe. The first time she opened her mouth, nothing came out. The second time, she managed a squeak. "Is Cam here?"

Ethan ran his fingers through his hair, instant concern etching deeper lines around his mouth and eyes. "No. Why?" Realization dawned in his eyes. Ethan pulled her to him and cradled her as if it were the most natural thing in the world. "I'm sorry. This is my fault. You told him what I said, didn't you?" He kissed the top of her head. "We'll find him, Holly. I promise. We'll find him. And I know just where to look."

Stepping in behind Holly, Ethan wedged the door to the barn closed with his shoulder and shut out the biting wind. He knew Cameron was here; the footprints in the snow didn't lie. He just had to find him. With a flick of his finger, the lone lightbulb in the center of the room illuminated all but the corners of the large space. He stomped his feet to remove the snow and rubbed his gloveless hands together. Despite being on the inside, he saw his breath. This place still wasn't ready for the dogs—or the twelve-year-old boy hiding somewhere inside.

Cameron. This time his words had put another life in danger. But he could fix that when he found the boy.

As he thought of decorating the Christmas

tree at Holly's house yesterday, memories rushed through his mind—the laughter, the friendship, the love. All the times they'd spent together held special meaning for him. Ethan grasped the reality of the situation. He loved the boy like his own. He loved the boy's mother.

Determination filled him. God had granted him a new day and another chance. This time he would seize the opportunity and not fail.

In the corner past the row of assembled dog kennels, Ethan saw the pile of blankets and towels that the church had donated. Amid the greens, browns and tans, he spotted an unusual lump in the center.

"This way." He grabbed Holly's hand and pulled her with him. With his heart beating a tad bit more than normal, Ethan made short work of the space between them. Cameron's pale face was a sharp contrast to the black beanie hat and the dark brown blanket covering him.

"Cam." Holly gasped in relief, sank to her knees and then reached out to touch her son.

At the same time, Ethan squatted and gently shook the boy's shoulder. "Wake up, Cameron. Your mom is worried sick about you."

After a few moments, Cameron woke up and glanced between them with a worried, nervous look. "Mr. P.? Mom? You're here?" He tried to dig himself deeper into the pile, his scared gaze never leaving Ethan's face. "My mom said you didn't want me out here anymore. Did you mean it?"

The saliva fled Ethan's mouth, making talking difficult. What could he say when the words were true? He stared at the stricken look etched into the boy's features. In Ethan's preoccupation with himself and his own feelings, he hadn't thought about Cameron's. Just like he'd only thought about himself and blaming himself for what happened in Afghanistan.

Let go, let God. It was about time he started not just listening to the words, but living them, too. "I've been saying and feeling a lot of things, and I thought it for the best after the accident yesterday. I'm sorry if I hurt you, but your mother spoke the truth."

"Then you don't want me out here? You don't need my help anymore?" Cameron's bottom lip shook as he clutched the blanket to his throat.

Ethan stilled. Help? He needed a lot of help. He couldn't do it alone. He never could. God was always with him and He always made sure that His children had what they needed. Sometimes it just took them time to figure that out. "That was yesterday. Today is a different story. You don't think I can handle this all by myself, do you?"

Cameron shook his head, hope blazing in his eyes.

Ethan stood and held out his hand to help Holly to her feet before he reached out for Cameron. "How did you get all the way out here?"

Wide eyes stared back at him. "I hitchhiked. I told the man that I'd run away from home and wanted to get back. He dropped me off at the end of the driveway."

"Cam!" Beside him, Holly gasped and stiffened.

Ethan wrapped his arm around the boy's shoulders and squeezed, careful of his broken arm. Things happened, despite all the precautions. There was no way he could have prevented the accident any more than what happened in Afghanistan. Peace finally settled within him. "We'll talk about the dangers of hitchhiking later. Right now we need to get you to a warmer place before you catch pneumonia. And if it's all right with your mom, there are some dogs that need some attention this afternoon."

After Cameron went to bed later that night, Holly pulled the old banker's box from where she'd hidden it in her closet. Sadness and anticipation filled her. Without opening it, she carried it downstairs, placed it on the coffee table and then rubbed her hands against her jeans.

She knelt, sank back onto her heels and then scratched Figaro under his chin. "Well, Figgy. Here we go. Are you ready?" Her cat rubbed the top of his head against her palm. She hadn't looked inside in a couple of years. After Jared died, she hadn't had the heart to set it out that Christmas.

All because of her inability to let go of her husband and let someone else get close to her and her son. Jared was dead and nothing would bring him back. She'd made peace with that. So what was keeping her from admitting her love for Ethan?

Fear.

Because letting someone else into her life opened up the possibilities of losing him as she'd lost Jared. Except there were no guarantees in life. This year, she'd found the courage, thanks to Ethan.

Taking a deep breath to calm her nerves, she lifted the lid and stared at the crinkled newsprint used to protect the contents. The article for the annual lighting of the Christmas tree in the town square caught her eye.

Life went on. As it should. For two years, she'd put everything on hold, grasping the memories of what she'd had and closing her eyes to her future.

Or what she hoped to be her future.

The paper rustled as she unwrapped the carved wooden animals first. Fingering the carvings, she marveled at the intricate whittling, even down to the texture of the lamb's wool. Jared had worked on these for hours while they'd sat and talked about their days, their hopes, their dreams. Back then, she'd wanted to be an interior designer, but life had a funny way of intruding. Maybe now that the shop was officially closing December 27, she could revisit that dream.

She set the animals on the glass surface and reached in again as her cat sniffed at the wood figures. "Leave them alone, Figgy." Holly shooed him away. Mary and Joseph came out next, followed soon by the shepherds, three kings and then baby Jesus and the manger. The last piece she took out was the stable that sheltered the nativity set.

She'd missed her mantel centerpiece.

A quiet knock sounded on the front door, breaking the stillness in the room. Figaro fled and scampered upstairs as she stood. Holly flipped the switch when she walked by the stereo but resisted lighting another candle. The five candles in the fireplace were enough and the Christmas tree already fragranced the air. She glanced up at the ceiling between the living room and front hall and smiled. Her last impromptu decoration was ready.

After opening the door, Holly admitted Ethan, took his jacket and hung it on the antique coat tree. He looked tired, but good. Now what? Should she just come right out and blurt what she wanted to say or work into it and wait for the right opportunity? She ran her fingers along the roughness of his jacket, gathering her composure. *Okay, Lord, I could really use some support here.* Turning around to face him, she fisted and unfisted her hands. "Thanks for coming over on such short notice."

Not exactly what she had in mind. Guess she'd have to work into it.

"Is everything okay? You sounded—"

"Everything is fine. I wanted to share something with you." Inhaling deeply, Holly wrapped her hand in his and pulled him into the living room, feeling more nervous than a schoolgirl at her first Sadie Hawkins dance. Then she motioned for him to sit before she handed him a cup of hot chocolate she'd brewed while waiting. Another Christmas carol hung in the air and the candlelight flickered, casting shadows against the brick wall of the fireplace.

Holly sat on the couch next to Ethan as he examined the figure of Joseph. This wasn't how she'd envisioned the moment, but then again, she hadn't had much practice in this area lately. Butterflies took flight and even a sip of hot chocolate didn't soothe them. Her fingers tightened around her mug. Maybe this wasn't such a good idea after all. Ethan seemed almost as uncomfortable as she felt.

"This looks like Jared's work."

"It is. They took forever to carve, but the five nativity sets he completed sold for a thousand dollars apiece. This is the last one."

"You're not going to sell it, are you?"

Holly stared at the set on the table, emotion hovering near the surface, begging to be released. "Of course not." She took a deep breath and flexed her fingers. It was now or never. It was what she wanted and knew that Cameron wanted as well even though they hadn't discussed it. Holly figured she'd better see where Ethan stood on the issue. "I thought you'd like to see it. And maybe help me set it up."

His eyebrows rose. "This is amazing. The detail is incredible, but it's small. I don't see why you need my help."

Holly was tempted to throw a pillow at him but didn't for fear of damaging the carving. Was he that obtuse? Or had she and Kristen misread him?

No. His eyes twinkled and his lips twisted into a grin that she'd come to associate with him. He wasn't going to make this easy on her. "Really? Then I guess it's time for you to leave. Thanks for coming by."

"Not until you tell me why you wanted me to come over after nine o'clock at night." He set the carving back down on the table and stood. Seconds later, he pulled her to her feet and held her close. "So are you going to tell me or do I have to coerce it out of you?"

He inched her backward.

Her fingers splayed across his shirt and she allowed him to lead, one baby step at a time. "Thanks for knowing where to find Cameron today."

"Holly, I—"

"Shh." She put a finger to his lips and stared into his eyes. "And for making me realize I need to move forward."

After he removed her finger, he gently kissed the tip of it. "You're not the only one who needed to put the past to rest. I had a lot of time to think about things in the hospital last night. With all my Bible studies, I should know that everyone has only a finite time on earth before they are called home. I did the best I could over there."

"And you continue to do His work by taking care of our service men and women's animals while they're gone and reuniting them with the strays they've adopted once they're back here.

Plus, you've worked wonders with Cameron. I think that's why you're here."

Ethan took another step back and dragged her with him. "He had his reasons, and I'm not the one to question it."

"I'm not, either. I realize now that Jared's time was done, but mine and Cam's and even yours still continues." Despite all her hardships over the past few months, she knew everything would be okay as long as she allowed God to remain a part of her life. Would Ethan remain part of it, too?

"So where does that leave us?"

Holly glanced up and realized Ethan had maneuvered her into the hallway, specifically under her impromptu decoration. "Where do you want it to leave us?"

"That depends." His head dipped down and his lips captured hers, and Holly returned the kiss with all the emotion and love she felt inside. "I like the mistletoe. Nice touch."

"I thought it might help move things along." She inhaled sharply. Ethan had awakened her, opened her up to understanding and forgiveness and made her want to take another chance. "I love you, Ethan." Holly never thought she'd ever utter those words again and yet she had no problem now. She'd managed to forgive herself and move on, and Ethan had done the same.

"I love you, too, Holly." He captured her lips again, bringing back her Christmas spirit.

Reluctantly, Ethan pulled away. "You know there's only one thing to do about it, don't you? But I'm not really prepared."

Holly hugged him around his waist. "Who cares about material things? It's what's in our hearts that counts."

A hesitant look flitted across the features Holly had come to love. "About the store—"

"Don't worry about it. That was Jared's dream. I have others. I've also decided that instead of keeping the woodworking shop locked up, I'm going to give the keys to Cam for Christmas. Those are the final pieces to letting go."

"That's a great idea. You are amazing. But still…" His gaze wandered past her shoulder. Seconds later, he pulled an ornament from her Christmas tree, strode back and got down on one knee. Maneuvering the ornament to the thumb on his right hand, he grabbed her left hand and pulled it toward him. He hung the small knitted wreath on her ring finger. "The physical therapist was right. It does get easier with time."

"Of course it will."

A smile lit his lips, yet she heard the seriousness and hesitation in his voice. "Holly, will you marry me?

"Yes." Tears filled her eyes again and a smile danced on her lips.

"So when do we tell Cameron?"

"How about Christmas? I think that would be the best family present we could give him."

"And that will give me some time to find just the right symbol to show my love. This just doesn't seem to be working." He picked up the wreath that had slipped from her finger and slipped it on again. "Maybe I can incorporate your birthstone somewhere in the equation. When's your birthday?"

"December 25."

"A Christmas baby?"

"That's why my parents named me Holly. It was the last thing my mom saw as they were leaving for the hospital. Apparently I wanted some Christmas ham, because I interrupted their dinner."

"At least it wasn't mistletoe she saw." He sneaked another kiss. "So do I still need to help you with the nativity set?"

"Of course. I'm not going to let you out of my sight that easily." She dragged him back to the coffee table. "We set it up on the mantel. Of course, we didn't do it until Christmas Eve, but somehow I felt the need to do this now. I think it's the final piece of saying goodbye to Jared but still keeping a part of him in our lives at Christmastime. You don't mind, do you?"

"Of course not. Jared was my friend and a very important part of your and Cameron's lives. What do you say we start a new tradition, though? We did this in Afghanistan. We put the pieces apart from each other and moved them toward the stable as we got closer to Christmas." Picking up the stable and manger, he set them on the mantel, positioning them in between the two small silk poinsettias.

Holly picked up the donkey and lamb. "So by Christmas morning, everyone will be together. Like us."

Ethan nodded, the love shining from his eyes enveloped her in their warmth, and she looked forward to many more years to come.

"The animals should be in the stable, shouldn't they?"

"Yes, and Mary and Joseph should be over here." Ethan placed them on the far side of the mantel.

"The shepherds would be on the other side?"

"You're getting the idea."

"But where should we put the three kings? They wouldn't even be in the picture yet."

"We can leave them on the coffee table unless Figaro would be a problem."

"Maybe we'd better set them on the side table."

Remembering the cat's curiosity earlier, Holly picked up the carvings and set them on the small table in the corner, where her cat wouldn't bother them.

"I think I'm going to like this new tradition." Holly dusted her hands and stepped back into the room so she could survey the scene. What they'd created was more realistic, and moving the characters each day would bring the real meaning of Christmas closer to their hearts.

Ethan reached for Holly and held her close again. "And I think I'm going to like creating new ones with you and Cameron, as well."

"You know what, Mr. Pellegrino? The future Mrs. Pellegrino is going to like that herself. She's also thinking another tradition might be to put mistletoe in each room, too." She wrapped her arms around Ethan's neck, pulled him closer and sealed her vow with another kiss.

Epilogue

Holly stepped out onto the back porch of the old farmhouse and handed a glass of iced tea to Ethan. She sat on the rocker next to him and breathed in the last of the warm scent of the lingering summer. The diamond flanked by blue topaz in her wedding ring glistened in the September sun as she took in the green splendor of the trees and grass. Puffy white clouds dotted the light blue sky, and the sound of chirping birds surrounded her. More peace settled across her shoulders.

"Thanks, Holly. May I offer you a cookie?" Ethan held up the tray of chocolate-chip cookies he and Cameron had made earlier while Holly rested.

The scent of chocolate drifted by her nose and she put her hand on her middle. "I think we'd like that."

"Is everything okay?" In a flash, Ethan was on his feet, concern overriding the love etched into his features.

"Everything is fine. I've been through this before." She smiled and gazed at her husband before she looked up. *Thank you, Lord, for bringing us together. For showing us that there can be life after tragedy. And for giving me the strength and courage to move on.*

"But what took you so long? I was beginning to think I'd have to do a search and rescue."

More happiness filled Holly. Closing the shop and putting Jared's dream to rest had allowed Holly more time to do what she discovered she really loved—taking old things and recycling them into something usable. "I just got another call about a decorating project over in Flagstaff. Apparently, the man saw what I did with some of the old stuff from the Weaver estate and wants me to rehab some of his things."

"That's awesome. Just as long as you don't overextend yourself." He looked at her stomach before his gaze rose to her face again. "There's something you're not telling me. What is it?"

"I also took another phone call from a staff sergeant who leaves next month."

"And you told him we were full, right?" Ethan rubbed his neck, his gaze frozen on the barn to their right.

"Of course not." Holly laughed. "We also just received another check in the mail. I think it's time to start renovating the loft and build a real staircase and ramp. We can probably fit about eight kennels up there if we really squeeze them together." Holly bit down on her lip to keep her laughter in.

"What?"

"Hazel the ferret is about to get some company. Two cats are coming with the new dog."

Ethan groaned and sank back down into his rocking chair. "I hope they get along with Figaro."

"I'm sure they will." The topic of their conversation padded onto the porch and jumped into Holly's lap. She patted him, resulting in a satisfied purr. "So you never did tell me why you don't like cats."

"It's not that I don't like them. It's just that I don't understand them. They're just so aloof, and what's with all the things Figaro is constantly leaving on the doorstep?"

Holly couldn't help but laugh this time. "Those are presents. It's just his way of showing you how much he loves us."

"Funny way to show it. Why not lick your face like a dog? Never mind, don't answer that. Those cats will be your responsibility, except for the litter box."

"Why, thank you, Ethan. I'm glad you're going to let me do something to help after all this time."

Ethan grabbed her hand, held it to his lips and kissed each knuckle gently. "Despite your role as a board member and taking care of the books, you've been a bigger help to me than you'll ever know."

"Patrick, you're not doing it right. Let me show you again." An animated Cameron and Patrick emerged from the barn. Two other at-risk youths followed them with dogs in tow. Boys and dogs. Ethan's idea to do youth interventions had been accepted by the town, and there was currently a waiting list to get in. With the added dogs and work, he'd be able to take one more boy and hopefully turn his life around just as Ethan's had been all those years ago.

"And everything has turned out just fine, hasn't it?"

"Better than I could have ever imagined, Holly. Better than ever."

* * * * *

Dear Reader,

I love the holidays; I always have and always will. I especially love Christmas with the lights, trees, decorations and music, and don't even get me started on the food. But Christmas isn't just about all the commercialism associated with it; it's about the birth of our Lord. The reason for the season.

The Christmas pageant scene in this book is taken from a tradition that our little town has done almost every year for over fifty years. And yes, just like Cameron, my son played baby Jesus when he was an infant.

Trimming the tree in our house has become another tradition with the kids and me. For the first few years, all the ornaments were at the bottom of the tree. Now my son, who is almost as tall as I am, has the honor of putting the star on top. Pulling out the ornaments the kids have made or holding that special ornament of that place we visited (yes, I collect ornaments from each vacation) easily transports me back to that time and all the thoughts and emotions that happened. Our tree is filled with wonderful memories and lots of toys for the cats to play with.

But holidays aren't always easy for some, and it can be a lonely time. The first year after losing a loved one is hard. So can the following years be, as our heroine, Holly, has discovered. So with the holiday season almost upon us, keep those people in your heart and say an extra prayer for them. If you are experiencing this yourself, please remember, as long as we keep the Lord in our lives, we are never truly alone.

Blessings,
Kim Watters

Questions for Discussion

1. Holly suffered a great loss when her husband died. Why do you think God allows such difficult things to happen to His children? Have you ever suffered this kind of loss? How did you handle it?

2. What do you think the appeal is for small-town living? What do you feel the pros and cons are between rural areas, small towns, urban settings and the big city? Does where you live affect your outlook on life? How?

3. Reflect on psalm 71:20, written in the front of this book. Have you ever been in a situation where this psalm would have helped you? Can you think of another Bible verse that might have been appropriate for this book?

4. What is your favorite character and why? Your favorite scene and why?

5. Ethan carries around survivor's guilt because people who depended on him died, while he survived. Guilt is a powerful and crippling emotion. What are some other things that guilt can do? How can faith help

you overcome that feeling? How can we help others who are faced with this type of emotion?

6. Holly has her own guilt about what happened the night of the accident. What are some of the things she could have done to help her through her husband's death?

7. Holly has continued to live her husband's dreams and not her own until she is forced to close down the shop. Do you think she made the right decision? Have you ever faced such a decision? How did you handle it?

8. Let go, let God. That is Ethan's motto. Do you have a favorite motto or Bible verse that helps you on a daily basis? What is it? How does it help?

9. The holiday season is tough on people when they experience the loss of a spouse or someone else close to them. If this has happened to you, how did you handle it? If this has happened to someone you know, how did you help them through the difficult time?

10. Holly and Ethan's first meeting didn't go well because of the trouble caused by her

son. Has this ever happened to you? How did you fix the situation?

11. Holly becomes afraid that her son will fall for Ethan and forget about his real father. She says she can't risk Cameron's heart, but what is she really afraid of?

12. Bullies are everywhere around us. Did Holly and Ethan do the right thing by going to the school and discussing with the principal? Have you ever experienced being bullied? How did you handle it? What advice would you give others?

13. What moral values are in this book and why do you think they are important?

14. How is God guiding both Ethan and Holly? What do they learn about each other and their faith?

15. How do the animals in this story help Ethan? Cameron? Is there a special animal or pet in your life that has helped you?

LARGER-PRINT BOOKS!

GET 2 FREE
LARGER-PRINT NOVELS
PLUS 2 FREE
MYSTERY GIFTS

Love Inspired®
SUSPENSE
RIVETING INSPIRATIONAL ROMANCE

Larger-print novels are now available...

YES! Please send me 2 FREE LARGER-PRINT Love Inspired® Suspense novels and my 2 FREE mystery gifts (gifts are worth about $10). After receiving them, if I don't wish to receive any more books, I can return the shipping statement marked "cancel." If I don't cancel, I will receive 4 brand-new novels every month and be billed just $4.99 per book in the U.S. or $5.49 per book in Canada. That's a savings of at least 23% off the cover price. It's quite a bargain! Shipping and handling is just 50¢ per book in the U.S. and 75¢ per book in Canada.* I understand that accepting the 2 free books and gifts places me under no obligation to buy anything. I can always return a shipment and cancel at any time. Even if I never buy another book, the two free books and gifts are mine to keep forever.

110/310 IDN FVZ7

Name	(PLEASE PRINT)	
Address		Apt. #
City	State/Prov.	Zip/Postal Code

Signature (if under 18, a parent or guardian must sign)

Mail to the Harlequin® Reader Service:
IN U.S.A.: P.O. Box 1867, Buffalo, NY 14240-1867
IN CANADA: P.O. Box 609, Fort Erie, Ontario L2A 5X3

Are you a current subscriber to Love Inspired Suspense books
and want to receive the larger-print edition?
Call 1-800-873-8635 or visit www.ReaderService.com.

* Terms and prices subject to change without notice. Prices do not include applicable taxes. Sales tax applicable in N.Y. Canadian residents will be charged applicable taxes. Offer not valid in Quebec. This offer is limited to one order per household. Not valid for current subscribers to Love Inspired Suspense larger print books. All orders subject to credit approval. Credit or debit balances in a customer's account(s) may be offset by any other outstanding balance owed by or to the customer. Please allow 4 to 6 weeks for delivery. Offer available while quantities last.

Your Privacy—The Harlequin® Reader Service is committed to protecting your privacy. Our Privacy Policy is available online at www.ReaderService.com or upon request from the Harlequin Reader Service.

We make a portion of our mailing list available to reputable third parties that offer products we believe may interest you. If you prefer that we not exchange your name with third parties, or if you wish to clarify or modify your communication preferences, please visit us at www.ReaderService.com/consumerschoice or write to us at Harlequin Reader Service Preference Service, P.O. Box 9062, Buffalo, NY 14269. Include your complete name and address.

LISLPDIR13